Throw Away Lives

H. Rad Bethlen

Rooster & Raven

Published by Rooster & Raven Publishing, LLC.

hradbethlen.com
roosterandravenpublishing.com

Library of Congress Control Number: 2025945244

For the Daughters of Zeus and Mnemosyne

Author Statement Concerning Artificial Intelligence

The way I write consist of several phases.

1. Idea generation.
2. Research.
3. Story development.
4. Outlining.
5. Writing the rough draft.
6. Editing and rewriting.
7. Editing and polishing.
8. Copy editing.

I will *occasionally* use AI during the research phase if I can't locate some bit of information on my own—but I try to locate it on my own first.

I will *occasionally* use AI during the story's development if I get stuck on something—but I try to resolve my own story issues first.

I *intentionally* use AI during the copy editing phase as a stand-in for a copy editor, which I can't afford to pay for yet which I don't want to go without.

A copy editor is the last set of eyes to look at a manuscript to check for grammar, usage, spelling, and punctuation mistakes. I ask the AI copy editor to make suggestions on corrections. I evaluate those suggestions. If I agree, I make the changes.

I don't use AI for anything else.

Be comforted that this story was written by a human being for other human beings.

H. Rad Bethlen

A Fate Reflected in Moonlight

Not everyone is born with the same opportunities. Some have it good, some have it bad. Some are born with the right genitalia. Some with the wrong. Some are born high while others are born low, into powerlessness, poverty, and everything that comes along with it: ignorance, hate, cruelty, and suffering.

In other words, the die is cast long before you get the chance to throw it. My own birth was to a low house, a subservient house, and I had the misfortune to be a male born after three females. Mine was a miserable lot from the start. The gods didn't do me any favors.

The light shifted. Esar-Haden looked up from his journal to the iron-barred window in the stone wall. He leaned forward. He could just see the curved edge of the waning moon. He was writing by its blue-hued light. He was a dark elf—a member of that war-making, subterranean-dwelling race, long ago separated from their peaceful, nature-loving cousins of the forests and plains—and could see fine by such a feeble glow.

He thought it ironic that the chill of the stone floor had caused the swelling of his left eye to diminish enough that he could now see out of it. The stone had made for an uncomfortable yet medicinal pillow.

The movements of a rat drew his attention. He kicked out, his leg irons scraping the granite. The rat paused, its dark eyes regarding him. Finding no cause for alarm, it resumed its search among the rotted hay. The air was fouled by its decomposition. Esar-Haden was already accustomed to the stench.

"For shame," he said, the scab on his upper lip cracking. He tasted blood and spoke with greater care. "I should not begrudge you the hope of a reprieve from hunger." He began to smile, thought of the scab, and didn't. "This is your home. I'm merely a shadow of a man passing through." The rat found a morsel, grasped it in its human-like hands, sat back on its haunches and began to gnaw at it.

"They got me," continued Esar-Haden. "I don't know how, but—" The rat turned an ear toward him but its eyes—and the majority of its attention—remained on the bit of stale bread.

Esar-Haden glanced toward the closed and barred door. He listened. Hearing nothing, he turned to his companion. "I didn't give up the gold." He laughed. The rapid swell of his lungs pressed against his cracked ribs. The pain wasn't so severe as to diminish his gallows humor. "Some shepherd boy will stumble upon it, long after I've been hung by the neck. He'll thank the gods for his good fortune! Little will he know."

He couldn't help but frown. The pain from his wounds, given to him by the Sheriff and his men, dampened his spirits, as did the thought of his gold—stollen though it be—falling into the hands of someone else.

"As for me?" He dipped his reed pen into the vial of ink sitting just to the outside of his right thigh. He held the journal steady with the first two fingers and thumb of his left hand, the others being broken. He had constructed a splint for them out of a scrap of wood he'd found in the dungeon—thankfully within reach—and a bit of cloth torn from his shirt. "I won't be bothering you much longer."

The rat regarded him. It licked the last crumbs from its fingers, turned, and scampered into the shadows.

What a Reflection Tells

Artain Geddes, high wizard in service to the King, one of many—his specialty being the school of transmutation, or the art of changed forms—paused upon entering the Hall of Mirrors. He was always taken aback upon entrance. It was an *environment*.

The ceiling and walls were covered by mirrors. They were not in gilt frames but fitted so that each mirror abutted its neighbor, making for a dizzying landscape of reflections within reflections. Even the white marble floor was polished to a reflective sheen. No rugs or pelts obscured its shimmering surface. Only the statuary, one perfect form after another, captured in white marble, set upon pedestals skinned with gold, dared block one's view.

Chandeliers of hooped gold hung from the ceiling on ropes of twisted silver. The light from forty pure-white candles shone from each. There were a dozen such delicate artifacts—with four hundred and eighty candles—running the length of the hall. Three men occupied their working lives trimming and replacing those candles, and in gathering every spot of dripped wax—before even a single offensive drop had time to cool and harden.

At the other end of the hall was a mass of men and women in the height of opulent fashion: furs, velvets, and silks, indigoes, reds, and greens, weighed down with precious stones and made gaudy with gold piping. All positioning—like well-mannered wrestlers—to get closer to the King.

They surrounded him, watching his eyes, judging the tone of his speech, mimicking his every gesture and word, always alert for a sign of his favor, always afeared of his disfavor. They did this because that's what the King wanted. That's how he controlled them.

Artain stepped to the mirrored wall and gazed at his own reflection. He was alarmed and dismayed, as he always was when he saw himself. Dull-brown age spots be-speckled his parchment-colored skin. His hair, what was left of it, had long ago lost its chestnut color and had become brittle.

His balding pate was hidden beneath a conical cap adorned with silver stars from which threads of gold extended like celestial rays. It made for a better sight than what lay beneath. His beard was white also, the tip down to his belt-line. He had begun to grow it in order to hide his age-sunken cheeks. He could not recall what his unshaven face looked like, so long ago had he begun his disguise.

The relentless march of time had been slowed, he knew, by all of the magic at his command. He had added decades to his natural lifespan. It was a victory, and yet, although retarded, the march could not be stopped.

"You're reaching up for me, aren't you, Arawn,[1] god of death? Reaching up from Annwn to claim—" The skin around his eyes crinkled as he spoke. "Pause your hand! They aren't ready yet. I need but a moment to keep out of your grasp!"

That portion of Artain's awareness not absorbed in morbid self-reflection noticed that the volume level in the hall had diminished. He turned just in time to see the mass at the other end of the hall part, revealing its glorious center—the King.

"Artain?" called the King. The mass began to approach. The King laughed and turned to those around him, although he gestured to Artain. "He thinks I've had

---

[1] Arawn is the ruler of Annwn, the *Otherworld*. He is a god of death and the hunt, and although he is often depicted as a fair and noble leader, here Artain expresses a reluctance to meeting him.

these mirrors installed to amplify *his* glory." The King's words elicit uproarious laughter. The King, advancing—his fawning entourage slavishly at his heels—turned his attention back to Artain.

"No, my Liege," said Artain, turning away from his own upsetting reflection. "But to show me," he swept an arm out to encompass the pack of courtiers, "to show *all of us,* your glory a thousand times amplified." This said, Artain hurried to the King, hurried with as much dispatch as his bad knees could muster.

An Artist Depicts

A young man, comely to look at, his chestnut-colored hair pulled back, his cheeks free of adornment, his eyes bright with intelligence and keen of aspect, stood before a large painting in the front hall of the *Elephant's Tusks Inn*.

The name of the inn was not originally thus, but had been changed. The King—his palace was near—had accepted gift of the strange, lumbering creature known as an elephant from a visiting monarch, visiting, it would seem, from quite far. The name change was in the beast's honor. It was also a form of advertisement to lure travelers to the inn and from that launching point to go forth to espy the elephant, after, if Fortune was kind, they had parted with an ample amount of coin.

The painting was of the young King and his court. The group portrait, of which this was an adept copy, was done to commemorate the King's coming of age and assumption of the duties of the office.

Although the artist's intent was for the King to be the focus of the viewer's attention, in this case it was another figure that drew the young man's eye. Although they were but smudges of pigment on a stretched canvas, the resemblance was unmistakable, especially to one with such exacting vision.

The door to the left of the young man opened. A breeze carried within its arms the mingled aromas of the outdoors, pleasant and rude. A stable boy, one hand still on the door, came to an abrupt halt. He hadn't expected his quarry to be standing just within.

"Horse is ready, m'lord," said the stable boy. "Tis but an afternoon's ride to the palace. She's beautifully seated, as ye shall see. The day's fine enough to please." The boy, having delivered what he knew to be an encouraging report, expected a pleased response. He received no response at all.

He studied the man before him, thought him to be too much taken with art, grew curious, then released the captive door and stepped closer to the portrait. He'd seen it before and found it both unchanged and uninteresting. He bent and attempted to read the placard beneath. At this he struggled, not being especially literate. The young man, his eyes still on the figure, came to his aid.

"His Royal Personage, the King, and his royal retainers portrayed as the gods and goddesses of the people. Painting by Jean Nocret."

The stable boy looked up to the speaker then once more regarded the painting. "By the Dozen King,"[2] said the boy, "I've never noticed they be gods and goddess, as such."

"The effect is subtle," replied the young man.

"Sub-tle," the boy tried out the word, "aye, that's just the thing for it."

"Any idea who that is?" asked the young man, pointing to the figure of his interest.

The boy squinted. "Can't say as I recollect, m'lord. Not being a part of that gathering, as such."

"No, of course not." The young man looked at the boy. "My horse?"

"Tis ready, m'lord," said the stable boy, the sting of disappointment in his voice, as he realized the man hadn't heard his report.

The young man produced three silver coins from his purse and handed them to the boy, whose mood lifted, as he was used to copper.

---

[2] Dagda, the ruler of the pantheon so shamelessly mocked, was able to separate himself into twelve distinct entities with no diminishment of his power.

"This way, m'lord, this way, if you please. Tis a fine 'morn, m'lord, finest." The boy pointed. "Follow the road and ye'll be at the palace 'fore lunch."

Faith & Fear

Brother Chulainn Callan peered into the lake's placid surface. Reflected within were the birch and oak trees that gathered round the clear-water lake, their edges blurred, the light that shone between their leaves sparkling. The reflections of diving and soaring birds sped across the water—darts of color and shadow. The grove was serene. His soul was troubled.

He glanced at the standing stone on the far side of the lake. He wondered how long ago the druids of the sacred grove—his ancient brethren—had erected it. The stone was tall, irregular in shape, carved with glyphs, and half covered in lichen and moss. He felt he should apologize to Morrigan, the goddess most associated with prophecy, to Cernunnos, in whose forest he stood, and even to Dagda, the wise father, for his doubt in them in their own grove. He wondered if he did doubt them or if he only wished to, for he feared what they had shown him—his death. He heard movement behind and turned.

"Brother Hugh."

"Brother Chulainn," replied Hugh, arriving at the edge of the lake. He looked to the standing stone, touched the pendant at his neck, bowed his head, and whispered a prayer. He looked at Chulainn. "You have spent much time here as of late."

"Morrigan demanded my full attention."

"Your divination?"

Chulainn nodded.

"Come, we must not beseech the gods overmuch," said Hugh. "Besides, our midday meal is served. Brother Sean made his raisin bread. And there is a hearty soup.

The smell of its simmering has disrupted my morning prayers."

"For shame," said Chulainn.

"My nose speaks directly to my stomach. There's no opening for piety to intervene." Hugh placed his arm around Chulainn's shoulders and the pair of druids began the somewhat steep climb to the keep. "My cleverness brings forth no smile."

"Forgive me, Brother."

"You worry," said Hugh. "Have faith in the gods. The knights shall find him."

Chulainn nodded but could not bring himself to smile nor speak. 'I fear they will,' he thought.

A Crow's White Feathers

Sir Gilroy tightened the strap of his saddle. He was a powerfully built man, a man of iron, for his long sword was at his hip, his shield and lance strapped to his steed. He yanked hard. His horse turned and looked at him but was intelligent enough to know that any protest would go unheeded.

He pulled off the leather glove of his right hand and ran his fingers through his dark, disheveled hair. He brushed down his mustache, and scratched the stubble of his square chin. He sniffed the air and looked to the sky. 'A good day for riding,' he thought, glancing at his campfire to make certain the last of the coals had cooled.

He reached for the horn of his saddle and lifted his left foot into the stirrup when the sound of beating wings, close by, paused him. He watched as a crow settled itself upon the saddle horn.

For a moment he was stunned, for the bird was practically on his hand. Being so close, and positioned almost at eye-level, it seemed a large specimen. He laughed at the bird's impertinence and was about to swat at it when the bird lifted its head to caw, revealing the patch of white feathers at its throat. Sir Gilroy staggered back.

He was a man of faith. A knight of the Order of the Silver Hand, serving the druids of the sacred grove under Lugh, god of battle. He believed in the power of prophecy and signs. He could even command some rudimentary magic and knew that the natural world was infused with a power well beyond his comprehension.

The crow lowered its head to gaze upon him with a steadiness of eye that was unnerving. Sir Gilroy took a knee and grabbed the pendant at his neck. He said a prayer to Morrigan, for he knew the crow to be associated with her. He felt she was speaking to him through the bird.

The crow shuddered, lifted its shoulders, bent its knees, fanned its pitch-black wings, then launched itself skyward. It cawed several times, the shrill sounds breaking the peaceful hum of nature, and flew above and beyond the trees.

"A portent," said Sir Gilroy, rising. "Of good and evil." He rose, grabbed the saddle horn, placed his boot in the stirrup, and launched himself upwards. With his heels against his horse's sides, and a pull upon the reins, he was off—his last peaceful respite behind him.

The Penitent Man Kneels Before His God

A steward, a dwarf by the name of Fagan Red-Banner, directed the young man into the Hall of Mirrors. He was one of the few dwarves in the King's service. He did not follow type; that is, he was not gruff of manner, given to profitless scowling, and had never once swung a hammer, neither at the forge nor in battle.

He was a man of refinements, who enjoyed the comfort of his station, who found the King's wine cellar a national treasure (dwarves were expected to drink only ale or mead), and who could quote any number of poets of reputation, and some disreputable ones, too.

"Name again?" asked Fagan.

"Keir D'Arcy," said the young man.

"You'd think I'd be better with names," said Fagan, peering over his shoulder. "Seeing as—" He realized that his charge was no longer following, but had been mesmerized by the otherworldly landscape of the hall. "A bit much to take in, ain't it?"

Keir turned to him. "Disorienting."

"Aye, 'tis that." Fagan motioned. "This way. Who did you say you were here to see?"

"I don't know his name," said Keir, "only that he's a wizard in service to the King."

"That narrows it down to a hundred or so," said Fagan, with a smirk. "What more can you tell me?"

"When he was younger he would have been well constituted—for one dedicated to book-learning. He would have had a natural athleticism and, unlike his peers, would not have demurred from the hardships of camp life, were he forced to it. He would have had a build similar to my own, hair of like color, and on the whole would have appeared somewhat like myself." At this Fagan studied the young man, as they were now walking side-by-side. "He must certainly be an old man now."

"Down to a few dozen," said Fagan.

"His athleticism and natural constitution have long ago left him. The loss wounds both body and pride. He's vain."

"Most wizards are," mumbled Fagan.

"And must be arrogant, given how much power he commands. He sees himself as above others. In many ways he is. He has the discipline of a monk but lacks the empathy. Most importantly, he's an expert in the school of transmutation."

"The school of what?" asked the dwarf, coming to a stop.

"A school of magic that alters the physical form—those of living creatures." He reached into a pocket and produced a folded piece of paper. He unfolded it and held it out for Fagan's review. "If he wears the obligatory wizard's robe it would show symbols of this type."

Fagan sighed, reached into a pocket, and withdrew a leather case. From this he plucked a pair of round-lensed, wire-framed spectacles. He set these on his ample nose and hooked the wires behind his ample ears. He took the paper in-hand, tilted his head back, and looked down through the lenses. He handed the paper back without comment.

"It seems you know your man, except his name."

"Deductions only," said Keir, "yet to be confirmed."

Fagan put away his glasses. "A gentleman comes to mind," he said, stroking his red-tinted beard as an aid to thought. "I can't say I knew him when he was young, nor that I know him over-well now." He watched as Keir put away the folded paper. "But if recollection holds, I've seen one or two of those fancy figures adorning his, ah, what did you call it, obligatory wizard's robe."

"Name?"

"Artain Geddes," said Fagan.

"What can you tell me of him?"

"Little more than what you've deduced." The dwarf continued down the Hall of Mirrors, leading Keir from one end to the other.

The hall emptied into what at first appeared to be a dark chamber. It was, however, a trick of the eye. There was too much light for the eye in the Hall of Mirrors and so it defended itself by narrowing the aperture. It took a moment for his eyes to adjust.

The room was paneled with a type of wood unknown to Keir. It was dark at its core but had a dramatically lighter veining, a natural display in the art of contrast. Various tapestries and gratuitously-framed paintings were spread about. Hung between these were the pelts of some of the more dangerous beasts of the land, including the pelt of what appeared to be a large cat, larger than a wolf, but with a pair of long tentacles that emerged from its shoulders and ended in pads adorned with both suckers and talon-like spikes.

Lanterns made of pure silver, shaped to resemble doves in flight, hung on almost imperceptible wires of gold. They appeared to hover. The naked marble of the Hall of Mirrors had given way to a multi-colored, intricately patterned carpet the likes of which Keir had never before seen. Cushioned, claw-footed benches and delicate, three-legged tables finished the room. A double pair of doors stood before him, from behind which came a dull roar of laughter, talk, and music.

"A moment," said Fagan. He opened one of the doors—sounds of revelry bursting forth—then slipped within, shutting the door behind him, returning the volume to a less offensive level.

Keir closed his eyes, slowed his breathing, and tried to release the stress that held his muscles taut. "Artain Geddes," he said. "It must be you." He opened his eyes and turned to the pelt. The tentacles, no doubt used to capture and restrain prey, were an apt symbol for this moment.

A door opened, the volume increased, and Fagan appeared. "The gentleman." He held open the door. Keir picked up a bit of dialogue from within.

"—visitor? He must be something indeed if he wishes to tear my attention away from you, my pet?"

Artain appeared in the doorway, a woman clinging to his arm. She was young enough to be his granddaughter, beautiful enough to be the prize of a knight's quest, and richly adorned enough to be royalty. She was, however, merely one of the Queen-Mother's handmaidens.

Artain and Keir locked eyes.

"Artain Geddes," said Fagan. "High wizard in service to the King. Keir D'Arcy, gentleman." His task fulfilled, he backed into the room and shut the door.

"Away with you," growled Artain.

At first Keir wasn't certain if he was being addressed, or the woman. She assumed it was her, turned, and vanished into the room from which she'd been led. The burst of sound upon the door being opened and closed punctured the tense silence between the two men.

"Speak!" commanded Artain.

"I judge from your reaction that I am not entirely a stranger to you," said Keir. "That confirms much that I had surmised." A *humph* from Artain added to Keir's growing certainty. "Shall I begin at the beginning or ask you what I've come to ask?"

Artain glanced to his right then turned and went to a bench, one opposite the displacer beast's pelt, with its limpid yet worrisome tentacles. He sat, his back straight, the palms of his hands on his knees. He did not answer.

"Was it you that placed me in the city orphanage?" asked Keir. "Or was that the cruelty of a lackey at work?"

"By my order," said Artain.

"A reckless choice, given how important I must be to you." This observation elicited another *humph*. "The priestesses of Brigid did what they could," continued Keir, "but, given how many orphans fell into their care, they were hard pressed to provide clothes, blankets, beds, and meals for us.

"We worked to provide for ourselves, doing the kind of manual labor that the nimble fingers of children lend themselves to." Keir held out his hands, revealing his callouses. Artain did not look.

"We children cared for one another and the decrepit, half-collapsed structure we called home. When our work was done we combed the streets and gutters like rats. A good day was one in which an extra bit of food was found, on a great day we saw the shimmer of a dropped silver, on most days we were kicked into the muck like the unwanted dogs we were. A pitiful life."

"You seemed to have come through," said Artain.

Keir nodded. "I learned early on that I was stronger than the other children. I do not only mean physically stronger, although in many cases I was. I was able to endure suffering to a greater degree. The pangs of hunger did not reach me as readily as they did the other children. Although I suffered the chill of those long, cold, winter nights I was not so miserable as those who huddled with me for warmth.

"I taught myself to read. I was even able to decipher a scrap of a text from Annwn, one whose meaning had baffled the priestesses. I accomplished this at the tender age of eight. It was my understanding of that scrap of text that drew the attention of Belcor the Mighty. Have you heard of—"

A sneer from Artain answered.

"He was far from mighty," continued Keir. "He was little more than an abandoned apprentice but he had one or two treatises on magic he was willing to lend. From these I learned the rudiments of the arcane arts. I cast my first spell at the age of ten. It was easier to survive after that."

"Then your time in the orphanage was not a waste," said Artain. "So you've a penchant for magic, eh? Is that why you—"

"We both know why I've come," said Keir. "There's no reason we should attempt to deceive one another. Is there? But let's not jump ahead. I've been waiting a long time to have this conversation. If you'll permit me?"

Artain smiled, but it wasn't a sign of encouragement.

"I began to wonder what it was that made me so different. How was it that I was not as ruined by poverty, starvation, and neglect as my companions? How was it that by the age of thirteen I knew more about magic than Belcor the Mighty, by fifteen more than the priestesses? How was it that the abilities of my mind and body, as malnourished as I was, were beyond those of the other children, beyond even the adults in my life? How was it that the unruly alphabet of Annwn was known to me?"

"Who knows why the gods—" began Artain.

"The gods?" Keir shook his head. "By the merest chance I stumbled upon a private club, one centered around a small library of obscure books. I befriended a member of this club and was given access—only after the priestesses vouched for my character. The members worried I would steal their books and sell them to buy food."

At this Artain chuckled. Keir continued.

"From this library I learned about transmutation. I can see from the gleam in your eyes that the school holds a special interest for you. Again, my suppositions are confirmed. I began to suspect what I was, why I was so different—so much better than others. And yet, who was responsible? Not the gods, no, they do not meddle in that way. But someone who had pretensions to godhood?

"So I began my search. I knew the man or woman I sought—I suspected a man, for obvious reasons—must be a powerful wizard, one talented in the art of changed forms. That's what I was, after all, a changed form. Or perhaps better stated, a perfect form.

"I despaired, for it was likely that the one I sought resided in some hidden tower, far from the habitations of man. But I deduced that no, he must be close. He could not leave my fate entirely to chance. He must be near enough to make periodical observations, to ensure his investment —for it's a most precious investment, isn't it, Artain—was not ruined by misfortune.

"I thought too that such a valuable vessel could not be totally unique. There's too much at stake for you to bet your own fate on one roll of the die, so to speak. No, if you were as capable as I know you must be you would provide for yourself at least two avenues of escape, if not more."

Artain clapped. "Bravo! You have proven your intelligence, resolve, and hardihood. What did you say? A vessel? You have proven yourself a fine vessel indeed. Was that your goal in coming to me?"

"I'm curious, what did you do with the others? There are only so many orphanages in the world. Did you deposit one in each?"

Artain laughed. "Are you so certain there are more?"

"There must be at least one."

"Must? Why so? If so, why not a hundred?"

Keir frowned. He was in no mood for games. "I'm not a fool. If I was alone you would have kept me close. You would have ensured my safety. So there must be others, at least one, as a back up. But transmutation is no easy school. It takes considerable power to alter even the smallest feature of a natural form. To do what you've done?" He shook his head. "Morrigan is said to change forms, but you—"

"The pinnacle of the art," said Artain, smiling.

"No pinnacle is easy to reach. No, there cannot be a hundred. Two, three at most."

"You think so little of me?"

"I think you great!" said Keir. "I think you powerful beyond my knowing!"

"And yet—"

"And yet—"

"You speak to me thus," said Artain.

"I know you won't destroy me," said Keir. "You won't close one of your avenues of escape, not without cause."

Artain began to rise, frowned, and sat. He looked at Keir. "I admit, you surprise me. What's the old saying? Man is least known to himself. Yet, here you are, and you've fairly well pieced it together. Annoying. I'm curious, how did you know I was here, at the palace?"

"I didn't," said Keir. "Not at first. I was coming here in search of aid. There are many powerful wizards here."

"Not as many as you think," said Artain.

"My goal was to question them. To lay my deductions before them and see if they could point me to you. It was at the *Elephant's Tusks* that I saw the final clue. It was a group portrait, one done decades ago yet still in fine shape. Within that portrait I saw a familiar face."

Artain laughed and nodded. "An admirable display of intelligence," his eyes narrowed, "and perhaps a bit of luck, too. The library. The painting." He smirked. "Your trial by fire has hardened you into a fine bit of steel. It was my hope. Well, you've told me much, tell me now, have we arrived at your question?"

Keir threw himself at Artain's feet, surprising the old wizard. "I'm prepared to do you any service, to perform any task, no matter how odious or arduous. I'm prepared to be your servant. All I ask of you is to choose the other. Will you?"

Artain threw his head back and laughed. "So that's it, is it? Treachery! Ha!"

"Not treachery!" growled Keir. "Survival!"

Artain clapped his hands. "This is all too much! And to think, for a moment I was worried. No, no, this will not end in servitude." He started to rise but Keir rose faster and spoke.

"It means nothing to you! What's the difference between one or the other? But it means everything to me! It means life!"

Artain glanced up at him, frowning, then commanded his old legs to lift him. Keir saw his struggle and grabbed his arm to help. Artain accepted the help, for he needed it. As soon as he was sure on his own feet he threw Keir's hand away.

"This has all been a waste of my time," he growled. "You came here to grovel? Pitiful! I expected more! Grovel all you like, you can't change the outcome. It's what *I* decide, when *I* decide it!"

"But—"

A door opened and the maiden from before, the one accustom to Artain's arm, rushed out. She glanced at Keir then went to Artain and whispered in his ear.

"The King has noticed your absence. He questions what's so important to you that you'd leave his side. He's genuinely hurt."

Artain frowned and looked at the woman. He turned to Keir. "Look what you've done! I'll have no end of groveling to set this right." He allowed the woman to pull him toward the half-open door.

"Wait! Artain! Please—"

The Knight-Errant

It was well that his horse knew the way back to the *Elephant's Tusks Inn,* as Keir was sunk in the gloom of defeat and saw not even the road passing beneath.

When the bustle and noise of the hamlet greeted him, Keir looked up. Those farmers and craftsmen who are wont to take their evening's meal at the inn were passing over its doorstep, the talk of the day on their tongues. A second traveler, coming from the opposite direction, arrived before the *Elephant's Tusks* just as he did. Keir only glanced at the man.

It was obvious he was a knight, although young. His steel breastplate shone beneath his green and silver tabard. His mail-coat jangled. On the front of his tabard was a silver hand, fingers outstretched, palm facing the viewer. His blonde hair was in a boyish cut, his face held a few day's worth of stubble, as soft as down. His eyes were bright-blue and seeking. His sword banged against his hip. His shield and lance were strapped to the side of his horse.

"Well met," called the knight. "Why such a sad countenance on such a glorious day? Egad! It is a most uncanny resemblance!"

Keir now saw him in earnest. "Forgive me. I was not —"

"I meant no harm," said the knight. "It's a most unusual thing, indeed." The young knight laughed. "And to see *that* face so troubled."

"Have we met?" asked Keir.

Both men dismounted. A pair of stable boys rushed forward to take the reins.

"Aye, sir, ye've returned from the palace already?" asked one of the boys, still aglow from the three silver given that morning.

"The palace?" asked the knight. "I go that way on the 'morrow. How is it?"

"The birthplace of tragedy," said Keir.

The knight did not know what to make of this. He could only knit his brow in response. Keir observed that the other man was studying him with some attentiveness.

"What is it?"

"Forgive me," said the knight. "It's only you resemble a man I know." He waved his hand. "It's nothing. I am Sir Abelard, of the Order of the Silver Hand." He undid the strap to the saddle bag, reached in, and removed a small leather pouch. This he tied to his belt. The stable boys led away the horses. The two men turned toward the inn.

"The men of my Order are on a quest," continued Abelard. "In search of a dark elf. We do not know his name but we have some particulars as to his person." He was about to go into detail but thought it unnecessary. "Have you, by chance, seen a dark elf in these environs?"

"A dark elf?" asked Keir. "I saw a dark elf some years ago, in the capital." He shook his head. "None since."

"They're as rare as the double rainbow," said Abelard, "rarer still." He grasped Keir on the shoulder and smiled. "It's no matter. He shall be found, for the gods will it. Friend, break bread with me. I would hear of the palace." He released Keir's shoulder. "If there's news of a dark elf anywhere, t'will be there."

"Forgive me," said Keir. He thought for a moment. "I, ah, lunched too well at the palace." He made a sour face.

"Rich, eh?" asked Abelard. "I shall be on guard. A knight learns to survive on what he can kill and what he can find. I've no stomach for sweetmeats."

"If you will excuse me," said Keir, as the pair entered the *Elephant's Tusks*, "I retire."

"May the 'morrow find you in better spirits," said Abelard. He watched Keir ascend the stairs positioned a few paces within the front door, just adjacent to a large painting. "Most uncanny," he said to himself.

A Turn of Fortune

My earliest memories were of pain and torment. The youngest of my sisters, Yolandi, was a sadist. She was trying to impress our two older sisters, who either ignored her or ridiculed her. Once Yolandi began tormenting and torturing me she felt powerful. Having superiority over me made her feel more like the other two, in her own mind at least. Whether or not my two older sisters thought more of Yolandi because of it, I don't know. I do know that they found my suffering amusing.

My two older sisters, Loci, the eldest, and Hydeia, the second born, had begun their studies at seminary. Our family was low born yet even the daughters of the low born are entitled to attempt the priesthood. Some demon might have a use for them. It was immoral to deny our demonic lords the chance to pick up a pawn when one was available.

Despite the inflated sense of importance this gave my sisters, it didn't amount to much. The best our family could hope for was to serve a more powerful and influential family, which, in turn, served some demonic lord. Even that dubious turn of fortune was reserved for the females. The fate of the males, of which I was the only of my family, other than my father, was to serve the servants of servants. A worthless fate.

One of my earliest memories came as I was learning to walk. I recall Yolandi kicking me in my ass and sending me flying. That sums up my life to this point.

Esar-Haden heard the clank of the bar being removed. He looked up from his journal. A feeble, flickering light shone within from the outer room as the door was opened.

"—alone?" asked a gruff voice.

"Aye."

"Entire time?"

"Aye."

A pair entered. He knew the warder, a crude man, fond of a boot to the ribs as a means of wakening. Although the second was unknown, Esar-Haden was troubled by the look of him, for he appeared capable and possessed a serious mien.

Sir Gilroy and the dungeon warder stepped to Esar-Haden, looking down at him.

"He writes?" asked Gilroy.

"Aye," said the warder. "Can read 'n write, that one. Smart, he is."

"A spell book! Did you think of that?" asked Sir Gilroy, pointing to Esar-Haden's journal. "All elves are skilled with magic."

"Some more than others," mumbled Esar-Haden.

"You were a fool to let him have it," said Gilroy to the warder.

"Aw, it ain't no spell book," grumbled the warder.

Sir Gilroy moved his finger to the reed pen. "He could kill with that."

"Huh?" asked the warder. "That twig?"

"He could have a lock pick hidden within," said Gilroy.

"There's an idea," said Esar-Haden, holding out the reed pen and looking at it. "You're right. I could just fit a pick in there." He shook his head, admonishing himself for not thinking of it.

"His crime?" asked Gilroy, ignoring the dark elf at his feet.

"Theft," said the warder. "From no less a personage than the King 'emself."

Esar-Haden looked up. "I'm no mere filcher of loose coins," he said, "it was—"

"Shut yer filthy hole!" growled the warder. He stepped up and gave Esar-Haden a kick in the thigh.

"Careful now," said Esar-Haden, reaching out to place the stopper in his vial of ink, for the warder's boot had almost toppled it.

"He's a lively one," said the warder. He grinned, revealing his yellow, uneven teeth. "Though not fer long. He's to be hung by the neck until he's dead." He looked at Esar-Haden. "Hear that?"

Sir Gilroy knelt and studied the dark elf shackled to the dungeon wall, the only dark elf he had ever seen. He glanced at the barred window and frowned, for little light came from without. The sole torch in the outer room offered little to aid the wan light of the recently risen moon.

He rose and stepped back, out of Esar-Haden's reach. He closed his eyes and mumbled a few words. The warder looked. Esar-Haden didn't need to. He knew arcane speech when he heard it.

A ball of pure white light appeared in Sir Gilroy's palm. He stepped up and knelt once more. "Lift your chin," he commanded. Esar-Haden obliged him. Sir Gilroy thrust his palm forward then yanked it back. He rose to his feet.

"It's true," he whispered.

"What's that?" asked the warder.

"His throat, man! Look!"

Esar-Haden once more titled his head back. The warder bent forward. "'Tis damned hard to see, it is. Black-on-black, as it were. Appears to be some sort 'o 'ritting." He stood and kicked Esar-Haden in the thigh. "What's it say, ye bastard?"

Esar-Haden sighed and rubbed his thigh. "It says 'Thrilled.'"

The warder looked to Sir Gilroy. "'Thrilled?' What do ye suppose that means?"

Sir Gilroy dismissed the spell. "Unchain him."

"Huh?"

"I said unchain him, damn you!" Gilroy looked hard at the warder. "I'm taking custody of him."

"Ye can't do that!" yelled the warder. "The King's men—"

Sir Gilroy grabbed him by the shirt and yanked him forward. "The King's men be damned! I'm taking custody! By the authority of the Order of the Silver Hand." He thrust the warder away from him. "Get the keys, and step lively!"

Esar-Haden rose and knocked the rotten hay from his backside. He reached into his jacket pocket and withdrew a chunk of stale bread. He searched for the rat but didn't see him. He tossed the bread into the corner. "Until next time, old friend." He bent and picked up his journal, blowing on the open page to dry the ink.

. . .

Sir Gilroy tied the rope that bound Esar-Haden's wrists to a stout tree. It was dark and he struggled with the knot, tying it by feel.

"Why not bring up your light?" asked Esar-Haden. It always amused him how helpless humankind was in poor lighting. It also amused him how meagre their sense of touch was compared to that of the average elf. He could feel that the knot was a poor one.

"Too close to town."

"Speaking of, why not stay at the inn?"

"Would they have a dark elf?" growled Gilroy.

"Why not leave me in the dungeon and stay there yourself? Couldn't this have waited until morning? Not that I'm not grateful."

"Do you always talk so much?"

"Only to those knights in shining armor that rescue me," said Esar-Haden.

Sir Gilroy walked a bit away, sat cross-legged, closed his eyes, and began to relax his body and mind in preparation for casting the most complicated spell he knew.

"You wanted to get out of there before the King's men arrived. That's it, isn't it?" Esar-Haden glanced the direction they'd come. "'By the authority of the Order of the Silver Hand,'" he said, quoting Gilroy. "Must not be authority enough, eh?"

Sir Gilroy scowled at him. "Quiet!" He closed his eyes and began to breathe rhythmically.

Esar-Haden twisted his wrists back and forth, loosening the knot enough that he could untie it with his fingertips. The rope slid free. He sat—not making a sound—rolled onto his back, and slipped his arms under him. He sat up and pulled his arms in front. He raised his wrists to his mouth and, using his teeth, worked the second knot loose, all the while watching Gilroy. It was a minute's quiet labor to loosen the knot. That done, he coiled the rope, set it aside, then leaned back against the tree, hands behind his head, and watched the knight.

He glanced at his gear—strapped to Gilroy's horse. 'Grab your daggers and slit his throat,' he told himself. 'Steal his horse and go get your gold. You could be halfway out of this backwards kingdom before dawn. You'll be as wealthy as you've ever been. One morning in the dungeon, awaiting the noose, the next morning a king in your own right, as rich as any noble in the land. Wine, women, and song await. Old man, why are you just sitting here?' He frowned. 'Seems a hard way to repay him, though.' He looked from his daggers to Sir Gilroy. 'What's he doing, anyway? An odd time for prayer. Pray before or after your clean escape, not during.'

He heard Gilroy begin the litany of a spell. He tried to guess the spell, or at the least the school, but he hadn't been paying close enough attention to Soléne when she'd tried to teach him magic. He was drawn to her touch more than her words. That was, he knew, always his problem with women.

Whatever it was, Sir Gilroy finished. He began to speak in a low tone. Esar-Haden, blessed with the excellent hearing of his race, could hear every syllable.

"Generous are the gods," began Gilroy. "I've found him." He paused. "Yes, I'm certain—the tattoo." He paused again. "In a dungeon—awaiting execution. I know, too terrible to imagine, and yet—" He waited, listening to a voice only he could hear. "Are you certain? He can't be trusted—" Gilroy sighed. "As you wish." He waited. "A fortnight, a bit longer, perhaps." Again Gilroy listened. "No, you're right, not at this hour. They'll be—" Some final command was given. "I will."

Sir Gilroy sighed, bent his head, and placed his hands on his knees as a preclude to rising.

"Secrets don't make friends," said Esar-Haden.

"Ye shall know soon enough," said Gilroy, rising.

"Don't be alarmed, I've untied myself."

Sir Gilroy reached for his sword.

"I could have gone for my daggers and slit your throat," said Esar-Haden. "That I didn't should tell you something."

Sir Gilroy relaxed. "We'll ride a bit further and make camp." He went to his horse and grabbed Esar-Haden's belt with its twin daggers. He walked to the dark elf, just able to see his long white hair and the gleam in his eyes. "Here." He held out the weapons. Esar-Haden took them and strapped his belt around his waist.

"I don't get your game, Gilroy."

"No man shall put you in binds while I am with you."

"Comforting, what's the catch?"

"I ask that you accompany me to our keep," answered Gilroy, "to the sacred grove that we protect, and to speak to our druids."

"That's it?"

"To find you and return you is my charge," said Gilroy. "I shall not fail."

"Well," said Esar-Haden. "It's better than the gallows."

Sir Gilroy could not help but laugh. "Do not test my blade, dark elf. I've yet to be defeated in single combat."

"How many dark elves have you fought?" asked Esar-Haden.

"None, but that may change."

"You're not all bad, Gilroy."

"Let's keep it that way, and it's Sir Gilroy."

Esar-Haden chuckled. "So it is. *Sir* Gilroy, my knight in shining armor."

Two Paths Become One

"Well met again," said Sir Abelard. "And good morning." Both he and Keir were awaiting their horses. "Here our paths diverge," continued Abelard. "I to the palace and you away. You are in better spirits?"

Keir smiled. "I needed but a good night's sleep."

"Which was had?"

Keir laughed. "Alas, no, but the late-night labors of my mind shall show profit yet, so I am encouraged."

Abelard smiled. A moment of silence passed. "I hope for news of my quarry," he said. "If I go in error to the palace, and if you should happen to spot him, I hope you will take pains to find me. He is the key that unlocks a great mystery."

Keir nodded his head. "A dark elf is no easy thing to overlook."

The stable boys arrived with their horses and each man alighted upon his steed. Again Keir showed his generosity, parting with a trio of silver. Again the stable boy, who was now twice enriched, beamed with joy. Abelard, parting with a single copper, produced chagrin. The two boys went away, bickering over the uneven distribution of spoils.

Sir Abelard settled into the saddle and turned to Keir, intent on a friendly word of parting. He was once more taken with the resemblance of the man before him with the druid he knew. He shook his head.

"What is it?" asked Keir.

"Take no offense," said Abelard, "but you bear a most unusual resemblance of one of the druids we protect. If you both stood before me I would think you brothers."

Keir could not hide his shock. "Tell me more, I beg you."

"His name is Brother Chulainn Callan. He is, as I've said, a druid of the sacred grove. It's at his behest that we search for the elf."

"What do you mean?"

"He performed a divination," said Abelard. "I do not know the particulars. The druids debate over those and over the need to confuse us with the shifting visions given to one who peers into Cerridwen's cauldron. Yet the dark elf is clear, as is the danger he poses."

Keir could not fit an unknown dark elf into the puzzle of clues which occupied his every thought. He did not know the elf's importance, nor could he guess. His focus returned to the druid Chulainn.

"Brother Chulainn Callan, you said?" Abelard nodded. Keir continued. "Was he by any chance orphaned to the druids?"

Abelard tilted his head in thought. "I cannot say that I know. I've only been a knight for a year, before that I was a squire for five years, before that I worked with my father and brothers on our farm. We give some of our crop to the druids every year. That's how I came to be a squire. I remember he was there from the first."

"Brother Chulainn, he's my age?" asked Keir. Abelard nodded. "And as you've said, we bear a likeness?"

Abelard laughed, "Remarkably so."

"I beg you, knight, break off your quest for this dark elf and take me at once to your sacred grove. It's of paramount importance that I speak to Chulainn Callan."

"That I cannot do," said Abelard. "Forgive me, but I've sworn to—" Abelard shuddered, as if some ghostly hand had reached into his being and frozen his thoughts by its touch. Keir studied him. Abelard's eyes glazed over. The tension in his muscles relaxed and he slumped forward in the saddle. Keir nudged his horse close, reached out, and grasped the other man's shoulder to keep him steady. A moment later Abelard sat up straight, but his eyes were unfocused and his lips moved as if he were repeating words overheard, although no sound came forth. A moment after, he shuddered and shook his head to clear his mind. He looked at Keir.

"What is it, what—"

"He's been found," said Abelard. "The dark elf."

"He's been—"

"I am to return at once to the keep." He paused, fitting the news into his mind and adjusting his course of action. He looked at Keir. "Our paths do not diverge after all."

An Argument

"The keep," said Sir Abelard. Keir followed his outstretched arm and finger with his eyes. The gray-stone castle stood atop a hill. Green and silver banners flew from its battlements. It wore pure-white clouds as a wreath and the sun shone down upon it. The canopies of the trees at its periphery swayed in the breeze. The twin oak doors were open, the portcullis up. Nothing more picturesque could be imagined, yet the romance of it was lost on Keir. His thoughts were of a darker cast.

"Behind the hill is a lake." Sir Abelard lowered his arm and looked at Keir. "There's a dormitory of sorts that the druids live in. At the edge of the lake is a standing stone, raised long ago by the men and women who founded the sacred order." He smiled and looked at the keep. "I was knighted kneeling before that stone, my right hand upon it."

"Chulainn is here?"

Sir Abelard nodded. "Come, I shall introduce you to him myself."

. . .

Chulainn could not look upon his twin as the pair walked from the keep, past the dormitory, to the edge of the lake. The druids watched them from the top of the path, astonished at the unexpected presence of a twin to one of their own. Neither spoke. Both were fitting the presence of the other into their understanding.

"It's as if I were looking into a mirror," said Chulainn.

"Yes," agreed Keir.

"I was orphaned," said Chulainn, looking at Keir.

Keir returned his gaze. "As was I."

"We must be brothers," said Chulainn, turning to look at the standing stone. "I never knew—"

"We're not brothers," said Keir. Chulainn looked at him. "We're the same person."

"The same—" Chulainn studied the man who could be his twin, thinking that perhaps his mind was touched. "I don't understand. What do you—"

Keir did not answer. He was organizing his thoughts. Chulainn returned his gaze to the standing stone and spoke into the silence.

"I've always felt—different. I—" He shook his head. "The druids have done everything they could have done for me. One wouldn't think them fatherly, and yet they have been excellent fathers, all. They've taught me—" Again he shook his head.

"They began to teach me all they knew. Even as a child I found their methods slow and inept. I only needed to be told something once to remember it. I only had to witness a spell cast to have command of it myself." He smiled.

"The druids were filled with pride—at first. I was the perfect vessel for their wisdom. But in time they grew wary of me. I was but a child and yet the most powerful magics they commanded, spells that had taken them years to master, came so easily to me that they couldn't help but be frightened. After all, I was placed at their doorstep. They knew not by whom. Could it have been a spirit that set me upon the stone steps?"

Chulainn cast his gaze over the forest of yews, oaks, and ash trees. He caught the flight of a bird and followed it until the bird was lost. "I can hear their chatter, the spirits, that is." He waved his arm. "This grove's full of them." Keir looked, but saw nothing unusual. "When I quiet my mind I can hear the gods conversing. I—"

"Can you understand them?" asked Keir.

Chulainn looked at him. "Yes. I can understand their speech." He looked back to the standing stone. "This is what troubles the druids the most. They're used to thinking of the gods as—mysterious, beyond human comprehension. To overhear them—to understand—is unfathomable."

Keir glanced back up the trail. The druids were still watching. A few knights had joined them. Keir turned back to Chulainn, ready to begin, but Chulainn continued.

"Ever since I was a child I've had a premonition of my own death." He turned and faced Keir. "I've been haunted by it. I've never known— I could never shake my fear of death. The druids tried to console me. The knights tried to grant me their fortitude." He smiled, then frowned. "Nothing has lessened this premonition. If anything, it's grown stronger. I cannot go an hour without the thought—" He blinked away his tears.

"It was there," he motioned to a yew tree. Keir turned and looked, then looked back to Chulainn. "Sitting there, under that branch, I performed a divination that I was loathe to perform. I asked Morrigan a question that I have been wanting to ask her my entire life—but was too afraid to. I asked her when and how I died."

"The dark elf?" asked Keir.

"Sir Abelard—"

"Yes, the knights—"

"Morrigan showed me a dark elf. I barely knew what one was. I thought it some kind of demon, with its ebony skin and white hair." He turned his gaze back to the standing stone. "He's the one that kills me."

Keir shook his head. "I don't believe that."

Chulainn turned, a puzzled expression on his face. He'd never known anyone to doubt a god.

"Artain wouldn't allow it."

"Who?"

Keir reached out and placed a hand on Chulainn's shoulder. "You were not placed here by a spirit. You were given to the druids by a wizard named Artain Geddes, or at least by his order. He ordered me to be placed in an orphanage in the capital, one run by priestesses of Brigid."

"Our father?" asked Chulainn, a hint of hope entering his voice.

Keir lowered his arm. "We have no father, no mother. No love-union created us—Artain created us."

Chulainn shook his head, not understanding.

"Artain Geddes," said Keir, "is a master of the school of transmutation. This school alters the forms of living things." He waved his hand. "From trees," he looked up, "to birds," he looked at Chulainn, "to humans. Nature is resistant to such meddling. Transmutation is a demanding school. Yet, when one reaches the pinnacle of this art, the art of changed forms, almost anything is possible."

"You think," Chulainn shook his head. "You think this man, Artain, *created* us?"

"Yes," said Keir.

"Then orphaned us? But why? It doesn't make—"

"We don't just share an uncanny resemblance," said Keir. "We're physically the same. We're the same person. We're Artain Geddes."

"What do you mean?"

"He created us, using his own form. We weren't born of a woman's womb, but of Artain's spell-craft. Ours wasn't a cradle of blankets, but of magic." Keir shook his head and frowned.

"He placed us as orphans because he couldn't be bothered to raise us. He has no interest in that, also, for what he's planning, it isn't necessary. All that's necessary is that we survive long enough for him to choose one of us.

"Then, when his plan finally comes to fruition it won't have mattered how easy or difficult our childhoods have been, what we've made of ourselves or have failed to. What we've become, who we are—it will all be gone, struck out, erased. Chulainn, don't you—"

"So it's him," said Chulainn. "He's the one in the vision, the one Morrigan—"

"What?" asked Keir, grabbing Chulainn's shoulders and spinning him so that the two men stood face-to-face.

"The divination," said Chulainn. "We—myself and the knights—we were fighting a powerful wizard."

"This dark elf, he must be—"

"An ally," said Chulainn.

Keir nodded his head. "Yes, some assassin that Artain—"

"No," said Chulainn. "*My* ally."

"You said he kills you."

"He does."

"Then how can—"

Chulainn reached up and took Keir's hand into his own. "Morrigan did not show me everything, only fragments. All I know is that a dark elf joins myself and the knights. Together we battle a powerful and evil wizard. Somehow, and for some reason unknown to me, during this battle, the dark elf kills me." He released Keir's hand. "The premonition of death I've suffered my entire life is now known to me. I sent the knights to find him—they have."

"Kill him!"

"They would," said Chulainn. "They begged permission to do just that."

"You told them not to?"

"I cannot change fate," said Chulainn. "Morrigan showed me what will be. It cannot be altered."

"No! It won't happen as you've said. I cannot believe that!" said Keir. "Don't you want to know *why* Artain created us? You said that you were the perfect vessel for the druid's wisdom. That's because you *are* a perfect vessel. We both are! That's our purpose. That's why he made us. We're vessels for him! For *his* mind!" He grabbed Chulainn's arms. "He's old. He's dying. He made us so that he can choose one of us to transfer his mind to. He's going to cheat death!"

"That's—not possible."

"It is!"

"But why two? Will he split—"

"He made two of us in case one died or became," he tried to find the right word, "damaged in some way—no longer perfect. He made a back up, just in case."

"What you say is fantastical, it's impossible to believe," said Chulainn. "Transfer his mind? It's just, it's not possible."

Keir released Chulainn's arms. "Think! All of the clues are before us. You can speak the language of Annwn. So can I. Who taught us this? No one. So how do we know it? Why does an understanding of magic come so easily to us? How is that we, who share the same appearance, were both orphaned? We've been separated and yet we're the same."

He spun and walked a few paces away, turned and rushed back. "When I was in the orphanage I was faced with hunger, cold, and hardships of all kinds yet they scarcely affected me. I have not a single scar to show! How could this be? You said that the knights tried to grant you their fortitude. You didn't need it, did you? You didn't need it because you *already have it*. Artain didn't just create copies of himself. He removed every imperfection!" Keir looked up the trail to the druids and knights. He turned back to Chulainn.

"They can't kill Artain. You can't. No dark elf alive, no matter how skilled with blade or spell, can harm him.

Nor can a dark elf kill you. Artain would never allow that. You said yourself that Morrigan only showed you fragments. What she's hidden from you is the truth!"

"You speak blasphemy—"

"I speak truth! You *must* listen to me, Chulainn. We don't have much time. We have to figure out a way to thwart his plans. It means life or death!"

"I know how I die," said Chulainn.

Keir spun away in disgust. He turned back. "Did the knights kill him? The divination? Morrigan? Did she show you who won? Does Artain Geddes die?"

Chulainn looked down then glanced at the standing stone. He looked at Keir. "He was alive when I died. What happened after—" He shook his head.

Keir tried to calm his emotions but struggled. "The dark elf, you said the knights have found him?" Chulainn nodded. "He's on his way here?" asked Keir. Again, Chulainn nodded. "When he arrives, you, he, and the knights will seek out Artain Geddes and go off to fight him?"

"Yes," said Chulainn.

Keir growled and started up the path.

"I cannot help but think of you as my brother," said Chulainn. "I do not know if what you say is true or not. I do not believe it. But," he held out his hands, "it really doesn't matter. Soon I will face him."

"You'll die, you know that."

"Yes," said Chulainn, "killed by the man who is on his way to me and who shall soon arrive."

"Then you're a fool!" said Keir. He turned and began up the trail again, but stopped when Chulainn spoke.

"I must thank you for coming to me," said Chulainn. Keir turned to face him. "It was going to be a struggle to find him. I didn't even know who he was. I was going to beg Morrigan to reveal him to me. Who knows if she would have. The gods have their own desires. I doubt they care about ours. But now that I know who he is, it will be much easier to divine his whereabouts."

Keir turned away in anger, stormed up the trail, and passed the druids and knights without a word.

. . .

Keir pulled on the reins of his horse, bringing it to a stop. The keep was just over the horizon behind him, the sun overhead. A thought had struck him with such force that he had been stunned.

"Damaged in some way," he said aloud, quoting his earlier speech. "No longer perfect."

He thought of the hamlet, that assortment of quaint homes that surrounded *The Elephant's Tusks Inn*. He went through a mental catalog of every craftsman he'd seen dining in the common room, every shop's shingle that had struck his eye. He remembered the barber's pole—a staff of white and red. He knew what those red stripes stood for. "A surgeon!"

He kicked his horse into a gallop.

No Longer a Perfect Vessel

Keir rode his horse to exhaustion. It took him the remainder of the day and most of the night to arrive back at the *Elephant's Tusks Inn.* He was sore beyond belief but leapt from his horse as if fresh, driven by emotion.

He left his horse before the *Elephant's Tusks,* not bothering to hitch it. The beast was too tired to wander off. The hour was too late for thieves. He ran to the barber's shop, also his home, and banged on the door.

After some minutes of rude banging, and yanking at the handle Keir heard a bolt slide. The door opened and a young woman's face appeared, illuminated by a single candle held in her pale, trembling hand. Her eyes were wide and she was shaking, so alarming had Keir's frantic pounding sounded within the house.

"Your father?" asked Keir.

"My father?"

"The surgeon? You must wake him."

The girl peered up and down the road, although she could see little in the darkness. She looked at Keir.

"What's happened? Is someone hurt?"

"Please, I beg you, allow me to enter. I must speak to your father."

"Let 'em in, sis," called a boy, whose face now appeared in the gap. He moved his sister with his shoulder and pulled open the door. He looked up at Keir. "Pa's upstairs, gettin' dressed."

The boy meant to imply that Keir should wait for his father to come down, instead he bound up the stairs. At the top of the stairs was a short hall with two doors, one open. Although the room was unlit Keir could make out two beds by the moonlight filtering in through the window. The other door was closed, although a flickering light showed from beneath. Keir opened the door and stepped in.

The barber, a man of middle years with blonde hair and a thick, blonde mustache, was pulling a white cotton shirt over his head. He wore trousers and was barefoot. The covers of his bed were turned back, the pillow a knot. There was no one else in the room.

The man looked up, astonishment on his face. "Wha —"

"Forgive me," said Keir. He went to the man and grasped his arm. "You're needed this instant."

The barber, whose name was Holenric Oates, was not as perturbed upon being woken in such a manner as other men might be—given his profession—although it was a rare occurrence. He was a little taken aback, though, by Keir's behavior.

"What's happened?" he asked, as had his daughter. "Who's hurt? My tools are downstairs."

"No one's hurt," said Keir.

"Then what," began Holenric.

Keir heard the children on the stairs. He continued anyway, despite the gruesomeness of his request. He released Holenric's arm and balled his left hand into a fist. "You must remove my hand."

Holenric looked at the clenched fist before him, then to Keir's face. "Remove—" He shook his head, thoroughly perplexed.

"Amputation," said Keir. "Have you performed such a surgery?"

The children, overhearing Keir's request, and curious beyond caution, entered their father's room. He glanced at them, frowning, but turned back to Keir.

"Once, on a calf with a—" He looked at Keir's hand. "Why, it's perfectly healthy. By the gods, why would you want it cut off?"

"I don't have time to explain," said Keir. He reached for the coin purse at his belt. His emotion guided his hand and the tie of the purse was pulled instead of the purse itself. Gold and silver coins tumbled out and clattered on the floor. Keir closed his eyes, breathed deeply, and tried to calm himself. He looked at Holenric.

"Are you familiar with the arcane arts?" Holenric shook his head. Keir continued. "In order to summon forth magic a complex litany must be spoken. In conjunction with this an intricate pattern of movements must be done with the hands. Some spells go so far as to require material components which are consumed when the spell is cast. If I have only one hand," he swallowed hard, "I cannot command magic."

Holenric glanced at his children then looked at Keir. "Why—why don't you simply refrain—"

"The choice will not be mine," said Keir. "I know my request is shocking but it must be done. Will you do it?" He held out his left hand.

"Sir," said Holenric, shaking his head. "You'll die. You'll bleed to death. Amputation is no small matter." He waved his arm. "A calf is one thing. A man, quite another."

"The wound," said Keir, "can it not be cauterized? To stop the bleeding?"

"Perhaps," said Holenric. "But it's not certain. You may still die, if not from a loss of blood, simply from the shock of it." He looked at Keir. "I won't have a needless death stain my soul."

"The responsibility is not yours," said Keir. "I have come to you with this request. The burden is mine." He knelt and picked up his spilled coins. He stepped to Holenric's bedside table and placed them next to his oil lamp. He poured out the rest from his coin purse. "Thirty gold coins." He looked at Holenric. "It's all I have. It's yours. All I ask—" He saw a look of uncertainty in Holenric's face.

"I don't," Holenric lowered his eyes. "I don't know if I can do so without causing a loss of life." For a moment there was silence in the room. Holenric's daughter whispered something to her father. He did not hear it. She glanced at Keir then spoke louder.

"The palace."

Holenric looked at her. "The palace?" He understood and turned to Keir. "Yes! Ryel Gynn! I did my apprenticeship under him. He's a far better surgeon than I. He's at the palace. It's a few hour's ride." He glanced out of the window. "If you leave now you'll be there by sun up."

"I cannot go to the palace! Not as I am!"

"Your clothes are road-worn, aye," said Holenric, "but Ryel won't—"

Keir stepped to Holenric and once more grabbed his arm. "It's not that. Argh! How can I make you understand? There's no way!" He spun and went to the bedside table, looking at the gold and silver. He spoke with his back to the Oakes family. "Although you cannot know it, this is a matter of life and death." He turned. "You fear my death. I understand. Know that my death is almost certain if this surgery *is not* performed. I risk death in order to save my life!"

Holenric looked at his children, then back to Keir. He sat on the edge of his bed. "This is beyond us, sir. We're simple folk. We've not got much learning and no idea of the arcane arts, as you've called them." He held out his hands. "I'm a barber. I cut hair and trim beards. I sometimes mend an animal that's gotten into the briar patch, or turned an ankle. I've castrated bulls and—" A gasp from Keir paused him.

"He had a lady on his arm," mumbled Keir. "No, it's not enough, not enough!" Keir went to Holenric and knelt before him. "Do as I beg, please. I will be in your debt." He motioned to the gold and silver. "I will pay you three times that, five times! Please, I beg you!"

Holenric turned away, unable to meet the fierce gaze of the man before him. Keir saw the answer in the movement and rose.

"It will have to be enough. A castration."

Holenric looked up at him.

"Thirty gold," Keir nodded to the table. "For a castration. Will you do it?" He could see that Holenric was uncertain. "Your daughter," said Keir. "She's marrying age. Have you a dowry for her?"

Holenric looked at his daughter. "A small one."

"If you do this for me, and if the outcome is as I think it shall be, I will return here in one month's time with a hundred gold for your daughter's dowry. It's a small thing to ask for so great a prize."

"Pa?" asked Holenric's son.

Holenric looked at his children, studying their faces, emotion clear in his. He glanced at Keir and nodded.

"Then it's done," said Keir.

"It's still dangerous," said Holenric, standing. "You can bleed internally. You could still—"

"I take full responsibility," said Keir.

"We'll have to do it downstairs," said Holenric. "We should really wait until day. The light—"

"It cannot wait," said Keir.

As they left the room Keir heard the girl whisper to her father, "One hundred gold, pa?"

A Second Confrontation

Keir had to borrow a horse. His was too exhausted. It was only because he had compensated the stable-boy so well that he'd engendered so much goodwill by it, that he'd gotten use of a horse.

If Holenric knew that his patient had left the *Elephant's Tusks*, where he was supposed to be convalescing, and that he was riding a horse of all things, he would be beside himself with worry. He knew that under such circumstances no stitches would hold.

The pain was excruciating. Several times Keir had to stop, lean to the side, and vomit. He stood in the stirrups while he rode until his thighs and calves burned. The horse didn't like the feeling of him standing and gave trouble. Only then did he sit, and only until the cramps relaxed. It took tremendous force of will to continue. Keir reminded himself what was at stake—everything.

He found Artain Geddes not in the palace, but beside it, at the stables. He was getting into his carriage when Keir pulled the reins and came to a stop. A footman was holding the carriage door. A driver sat atop. A stable-boy held the bridle and stroked the horse's neck. A guard stood at the palace door, the head of his halberd shining in the newly risen sun. The air was crisp. Dew was still upon the grass. They all turned to him.

"You again," growled Artain.

Keir dismounted with great care. He collapsed to his knees when his feet touched the ground. The pain reached upwards from his groin into his chest.

"What's wrong with you?" asked Artain. He was disturbed by Keir's smile and the vengeful gleam in his eyes. Keir struggled to his feet and staggered to Artain.

"What's wrong with me?" He laughed. "Is my color off, eh? Are my eyes sunken? Do I look unwell? Is that it?"

Artain frowned. "What's this, then? Do you feign madness? Do you think—"

Keir reached the carriage and fell against the side. The footman stepped away, uncomfortable with Keir so close. Artain looked up, for he was still seated, half within, half without the carriage.

Although Keir could easily reach out and grab him, Artain had no fear for his person. Keir had no visible weapons. If it came to a contest of magic Artain was confident he would come to no harm at all. Besides, he noted, it appeared that Keir hovered on death's doorstep. That *did* trouble him.

"Well, what is it?" barked Artain. "What do you want?"

"I found him," said Keir. "The other." He laughed. "We're exactly alike."

Artain smiled. "I should think so."

"Druids?" asked Keir. "A beautiful country seat? Me to the slums?"

Artain shrugged his shoulders. "I'm curious, did it make a difference?"

Keir did not answer. "I have secrets, Artain. Information you need."

Artain sat back, half-disappearing into the carriage. "You know what I need from you. I need nothing else."

"Yes, that's it, isn't it? A perfect vessel? That's what you need? That's what you've made."

Artain leaned out of the carriage and smiled.

"But have your vessels *remained* perfect? You should have kept us close, Artain. You should have raised us as if we were your own sons. You could have had servants do it. Then you could have prevented any—mishaps."

The smile left Artain's face. "You've come to tell me what I am to do? Me? Whose intellect and power you cannot even fathom? Me—"

"I *can* fathom it, Artain! Because I'm you!"

Artain glanced at the footman, then at the guard. "A madman," he said, motioning to Keir. "Spouting drivel." He looked up at the driver. "Ready your whip." He looked at Keir. "You're soon to put it across this fool's backside."

Keir stepped away from the carriage. "Is this what you want, Artain? Do you wish me to stay out of your sight until the moment you decide? To remain quiet and still, like an urn, waiting to be filled with your ashes?"

"Better that than this—scene," growled Artain.

"I can wait, Artain." Keir laughed, then coughed. He tasted blood. He wiped it from his lips with his sleeve. "I can wait, as untroubled as an urn. I have that power now." He looked from the blood on his sleeve to Artain. "Would you like to know why?"

"I tire of you," said Artain, pulling his leg into the carriage. "The door," he growled. The footman stepped up and grabbed the door.

"Because I know your choice," said Keir. "You've only one perfect vessel left."

Artain reached out and stopped the motion of the door. "What's this?"

"She's lovely, the Queen-Mother's handmaiden. Have you had her?"

Artain stepped out of the carriage, taking the footman's proffered arm.

"What's this?"

"A fan of bedding maidens, are you?" asked Keir, laughing. He coughed again. Blood again. He grew lightheaded and reached out to steady himself but there was nothing to steady himself against. He staggered and bent double. He coughed more, pain wracking his body.

Finally, he was able to stand upright. "Imagine, Artain, how many maidens you'll be able to seduce when you've turned in that ancient husk for—" He could not continue, the pain brought him to his knees.

Artain went to him, grabbed a handful of his hair, and yanked his head back. "Say more!"

"Castration," whispered Keir. "I hear that it lessens the pleasure of sex."

"You wouldn't," growled Artain. "You wouldn't do something so stupid."

"I feel sorry for him," said Keir, the vengeful gleam leaving his eyes. "He thinks of me as a brother. I had no choice. He left me none—you left me none."

Artain threw Keir's head back. Keir toppled over. Artain turned and went to the carriage door. He turned back to Keir, who had risen to an elbow. "A trifle," he said, waving a dismissive hand. "A moment's work, a few words of power and a bit of powdered carbuncle and all will be set right." He laughed. "A valiant attempt. I commend you. You truly are the better of the two."

"Ryel Gynn," said Keir. "He's going to amputate my hand." Keir held up his left hand.

"He will not!"

"I'll stop at nothing to defy you!"

Artain, threw his shoulders back, raised his voice, spoke a few words in the tongue of the *Otherworld,* and pointed a finger at Keir. A lash of crackling blue-black energy leapt out of his fingertip and struck Keir. He fell backwards, his body convulsing, electricity running up and down. The lash of magic dissipated. Keir went limp and lay motionless. Artain balled his fist and cursed at himself, for he could have killed.

"Fool!" he cried. "Damn fool!" He reached into his robe and produced a small, stoppered vial containing an iridescent red liquid. He waved over the footman and held the vial out. "Pour this down his gullet. Go!"

The footman did as ordered, uncorking the vial, taking Keir's limp body onto his thighs, tilting his head back, and administering the healing potion.

"I never imagined I'd have as much trouble as this," growled Artain. He produced a second potion and threw it to the footman. "Put that in his pocket. If he has any sense at all he'll—" He waved a dismissive hand, climbed into the carriage, and yelled up at the driver. "Get me away from this fool."

. . .

Fagan Red-Banner looked down into the drive from a second story window. He had seen it all, had witnessed the entire shameful scene. He had watched as Artain attacked Keir, laying him low with that lash of magic.

"Why?" he asked himself. He gave one last look at Keir. The footman, stable-boy, and guard were all standing over him, looking down, puzzled as to what to do. He turned and hurried outside, before anything worse befell the young man.

The Injured Parties

As the heavy oak doors were opened and the portcullis raised, Sir Gilroy and Esar-Haden rode into the courtyard unobstructed. It was mid-morning. The sun had just risen above the battlements. The day was fair, the sky clear, and the sounds of the forest grove carried on the breeze.

The courtyard, although cramped, was full of activity. A pair of men battled with wooden swords, hens dodging their feet. A boy was drawing water from a well, pouring the contents of the bucket into a shallow trough from which a pair of pigs drank. A man in dirt-stained trousers with a ragged cap atop his head led a bow-legged cow to a scattering of hay. A second cow followed of its own free will.

There were no women in sight. Only men and boys labored and played. Esar-Haden scanned the courtyard and the inner walls. He saw an older but powerfully built man wearing a green and silver tabard with a silver hand emblazoned on its front. The man stood with an elderly figure who had a long white beard and bright eyes, dressed in a white robe with a silver torc around his neck. They watched the pair enter from a balcony, their faces firmly set.

Both Sir Gilroy and Esar-Haden dismounted. Gilroy's fellow knights greeted him with cheers, hearty hugs, and slaps on the back that lifted the dust of the road from his green and silver cloak. It was a moment of victory, for the knights had succeeded in their quest. Sir Gilroy was the man of the hour.

These same knights, and those servants, squires, and pages in the courtyard, all eyed Esar-Haden with a mixture of awe and fear. A boy came and took the reins of his horse, whispering, "A dark elf? A dark elf!"

After the excitement of the arrival died down, Sir Gilroy turned to Esar-Haden. He stood with a group of knights, all men like him, men of iron. Esar-Haden stood alone. Not even the shaggy-haired, filthy dogs that ran free would approach him. He could sense the thoughts of the knights who assessed him. They were pleased and dismayed, worried and excited.

"Sir Gilroy," called the man in the tabard from the balcony above. Gilroy looked up. The man indicated with a movement of his head that he wished Gilroy to take control of his charge and to come up. Gilroy, understanding, motioned to Esar-Haden. They ascended a stone staircase and turned to walk along the inner balcony.

Sir Gilroy opened a door and stepped in. Esar-Haden followed. It was a small room with a bed, table, and chair. A narrow armoire stood opposite the bed.

"Boy!" called Sir Gilroy through the still-open door. A page appeared. "Scour the keep and find a set of clothes to fit him." Sir Gilroy indicated Esar-Haden. The page nodded and disappeared from the doorway. "Boy!" yelled Sir Gilroy. The page reappeared. "And water, so he can wash his face." Once more the boy disappeared.

Sir Gilroy went to the window and gazed down into the forest grove. He caught the glint of the sunlight from the lake's shimmering surface. He stepped aside and motioned that he wished Esar-Haden to come look. He did.

"Our grove," said Gilroy. "You can't see it from here, but our standing stone is just there." He pointed. "A beautiful sight, isn't it?"

Esar-Haden looked at his companion, then back to the grove. "I see why you wish to preserve it."

"Aye," agreed Sir Gilroy. "Truly the spirits play within." He walked to the armoire. "Rid yourself of that armor," he said, opening the door. Esar-Haden turned his attention back to the room. "If you'd be so kind as to leave your daggers here. Don't worry, no harm shall come to you within these walls. Nor are there thieves among us."

Esar-Haden undid his belt and set it on the table, the daggers clattering. He sniffed the air. "That wonderful aroma?"

Sir Gilroy smiled. "We eat well here, as shall you." He stepped to Esar-Haden and helped with one of the hard-to-reach straps of his leather armor. This done he went to the door. "The boy will return presently." He started out of the door but paused. "In truth," he said, speaking over his shoulder. "I hoped not to find you. I hoped none would." He half turned and looked at Esar-Haden. "I hoped you did not exist."

Esar-Haden smiled. "Sometimes I wish that myself."

Sir Gilroy stepped out onto the balcony, shutting the door behind him.

. . .

I was beaten and tortured, degraded and abused. I attended my older sisters in whatever way they wanted. Yolandi's favorite treatment was to force me to rub her feet, legs, butt and breasts with oil. She relished in my touch. She could feel how uncomfortable I was and how much I longed to be far away from her. She liked touching me, touching me and giggling at my discomfort.

My two older sisters didn't go in for such luxuries, not provided by me anyway. They ignored me, for the most part. Occasionally, one or the other would feel the stress of their forced lifestyle and I would happen upon them at an inopportune time. Then I would receive a beating or be taken to the torture chamber for a scene.

This went on until I was old enough to be trusted to act on my own. I was forced to run errands and start doing the small jobs that my sisters felt were beneath them. I preferred being in the streets to being at home. It was on the streets of Pwyll that I met other boys like me. I didn't find sympathy on the streets, even among boys who suffered as I did.

The dark elf language doesn't have a word for sympathy, nor do the hearts of dark elves have room for it. I did find a certain camaraderie. We all shared the experience of our class, station, and sex. While we weren't kind or loving to one another we provided some small comfort on account of us understanding our shared plight.

The older boys, some of whom had begun training at the martial academy, acted like our learned elders and we treated them as such. These boys spoke of their various escapades, whether real or invented, and this cast a spell on us younger boys, especially me. I always went in for tales of daring, thieving, and adventure. I think it was these early tales that impressed upon me the desire to be a thief and an adventurer, as there didn't seem to be a freer type of living and that's what I wanted, to be free.

No matter what I wanted there wasn't any freedom to be had. I had to go back home and do as my sisters commanded. My mother—in case you are curious why I haven't mentioned her yet —was a stranger to me. I rarely saw her except in passing. Even then I dare not be caught looking at her or it would be my death. I was not allowed to speak to her. I'm certain that if she had ever heard my voice directed at her, I would have spent the rest of my miserable life in the family dungeon.

She was a priestess and although she was low ranking and of little importance she was still a priestess. She spent most of her time trying to please and impress those above her, who were in turn trying to please their demonic lords. When she wasn't involved in this charade of a religion, she was making sure her daughters were doing as well as they could in seminary. By this time Yolandi was attending as well.

My father, a man I had seen perhaps three times in my life up to that point, was, like most males, in the military. The military was a tool of the priesthood. They were sent far and wide to fight on behalf of one demon or another. To settle some grudge or to start a new one. If I was a proper son and did as I was told, I would follow in my father's footsteps and get myself killed on behalf of some Abyss-spawned beast who would have no knowledge of me or my sacrifice whatsoever.

Are you surprised that I didn't go in for such a fate? Sadly, I saw no way to escape it. I was still just a boy and although I had never had the luxury of a boyhood, like surface dwellers were accustom to, I still had the mindset and sensitivities of a child. All of that would be ground out of me soon enough.

. . .

There was a knock at the door. It opened. Sir Gilroy stepped within. "Preparing a spell?" he asked, motioning to the book set upon Esar-Haden's thighs. By now his fingers, and the rest of his wounds, had healed, although his left hand was still tender.

He was half-reclined on the bed. He turned and set his journal open-faced on the table. He sat up and placed the stopper into the vial of ink. "One needs to be prepared for anything," he said as he wiped clean the tip of his reed pen.

"I wouldn't think of working magic here," said Gilroy. "The druids—" He stopped short of a warning, for he had seen the mischievous smile play across the dark elf's face. "You jest?"

"Aren't I a guest here? Aren't your people known for their hospitality?" Esar-Haden stood and smoothed the green and silver tabard. "Do I not wear the costume of the Order of the Silver Hand?"

"You talk so much, you must have an appetite." Sir Gilroy motioned with his head. "We eat." Esar-Haden rose and prepared to follow Sir Gilroy. He was surprised when the knight stopped him and felt around his belt, front and back.

"You think I hide a dagger?"

Sir Gilroy nodded.

"It's in my boot," said Esar-Haden.

Sir Gilroy started to bend but stopped and stood erect. He knocked his fist against the dark elf's chest. "Come on then."

The two men left the room, made their way around the balcony to the opposite side of the keep, and stopped before a closed door. Gilroy knocked. There was a call from within and he opened the door.

It was a rectangular room with a table that seated eight. Tall-backed chairs surrounded it. The table was set with plates, mugs, and cutlery. A group of druids, all but one wearing light blue robes, and a handful of knights all stood at the other end of the room. It appeared that they were surrounding one who was seated, looking at him, and—given the confusion of simultaneous speech—arguing with him. When Sir Gilroy and Esar-Haden entered they ceased speaking and turned.

The sole druid in white, the elderly man with the silver torc around his neck, motioned and half the men left the room, filing past Esar-Haden with looks of suspicion and worry on their faces.

"Sit," commanded the older knight who stood beside the druid in white. The man came toward Esar-Haden, his features hard. For a moment Esar-Haden tensed, expecting some harm, but the man walked before him, grabbed the back of the chair at that end of the table and pulled it out. He looked expectantly at Esar-Haden, who now sat.

"I am Sir Reginald," said the man, as he went to the other end of the table and pulled out that chair. The druid in white sat. "This is Brother Daveth." The druid nodded to Esar-Haden. Sir Reginald continued, pointing to a knight, "Sir Jory." The knight nodded, as did Esar-Haden. "Sir Ervan." Again an exchange of acknowledgement. "Brothers Lewis and Darren." He looked. "Sir Gilroy you know." Everyone sat, Gilroy to Esar-Haden's right, Brother Darren to his left. Sir Reginald sat to the right hand of Brother Daveth, the highest ranking druid of the order.

Esar-Haden now saw that a fourth druid, a young, handsome man with long chestnut brown hair and clean cheeks sat in a chair by the window, gazing down at the fields below. He was not introduced.

A stream of pages entered, carrying dishes, which they sat at the center of the table. One carried a pair of pitchers and filled each mug with beer. The knights and druids, neglecting to stand on ceremony, began to fill their plates. Esar-Haden didn't wait to be invited. He hadn't eaten this well in months. His mouth was already salivating. The presence of cutlery was lost on them, all ate with their fingers. A fair bit of the feast was consumed before much talk began.

Esar-Haden kept an eye on the druid not at the table. He appeared to be lost in thought and did not stir. His chin was in his palm, his elbow on the window's sill.

"We," said Brother Daveth, "none of us, have ever seen a dark elf." He paused and glanced over his shoulder at the young druid seated behind him. His words had caused no response and so he continued, turning back to Esar-Haden. "We know nothing of your people. Perhaps you can enlighten us. I believe your people live beneath the earth?"

Esar-Haden took a drink of beer, finding it well brewed. He set his mug down. "Yes, we're darkness dwellers."

"Caves?" asked Sir Reginald.

Esar-Haden nodded. "The city I'm from, Pwyll, consists of three caves arranged roughly one on top of the other. The central cave is the largest, the lowest cave the smallest. That cave, we call it Maljamir, contains a magical portal—a rift between the planes—that links our world to the Abyss." The eyes of the druids went wide. "You've heard of it?" asked Esar-Haden.

"We fear it," said Brother Darren.

"You should. A handful of demons have found their way through this rift and have taken up residence in Maljamir. They rule our city, making slaves of us." He laughed. "It's almost as bad as it sounds. Our society is not at all organized like yours. We've no laws, for instance."

"No laws?" asked Sir Reginald.

Esar-Haden shook his head. "Only the law of strength. Pwyll is organized into family houses. These houses all battle one another for supremacy. I imagine all dark elf cities, big or small, are organized along such lines.

Those I've been to all shared these characteristics. Not many other dark elf cities have resident demons, though, ours is singularly blessed in that respect, but almost all dark elves worship demons or the evil gods.

"Unlike your society ours is matriarchal. This division of power along lines of sex is absolute and viciously enforced. Males are considered property, if they're considered at all. We're expected to serve and to die—nothing more.

"We are a people without any traditions, moral or otherwise. Our society must certainly blow apart and descend into total anarchy, one would think. It's saved by only one thing—the will of the matron mothers. They desire some semblance of order so that they may enjoy life's pleasures. If it were not for our greed, lust, and gluttony we would all have killed each other long ago."

The knights and druids looked at one another.

"It has been our pleasure," said Brother Daveth, "to have known a few elves in our time here. These elves are the exact opposite of what you describe. They are nature-loving, peaceful to the point of serenity, and austere in their manners and desires. How is it that you, who are certainly cousins, are so different?"

"There are various myths," said Esar-Haden. "Most of them make us, the dark elves, out to be the victims of betrayal or of misfortune. I can't say I believe any of them. At some point in our shared history we split. Half of us went to the light, half to the dark.

"They—surface elves, I mean—embody light and all that it promises: truth, warmth, and life. We went into the shadows and embody everything it promises: lies, cold-hearts, and death. I don't know why this split occurred. But it did."

Again the knights and druids looked among each other. Esar-Haden glanced at the silent druid by the window. He had not stirred and was still, by all appearances, lost in thought.

Brother Lewis broke the silence. "Given the rarity of dark elves on the surface, your race must wish to remain below. How is it that you came to leave Pwyll to walk among men?"

Esar-Haden smiled. Thinking of his past always filled him with mixed emotions. "An attempt was made to conquer Pwyll. You see, we have no real economy, no commerce, no agriculture or husbandry, no crafts or trade —not really. We're a parasitic people. We live by taking the fruits of others' labors. We had been raiding the surface for years.

"Finally the town of Seven Rivers, and the ranches and hamlets nearby, had enough. For years pleas had been sent to the King to do something. He could no longer ignore them. The parasite was close to killing the host. Our continued existence was proving an embarrassment to the throne.

"An army was sent out. I played no small part in thwarting the fall of Pwyll. A male was never supposed to rise to such an occasion. Although grateful, the matron mothers hated the sight of me. I reminded them that they, the powerful women who ruled Pwyll, had failed and I, a male from a lowly house, had succeeded. After the third assassination attempt I decided that I'd better find a new home. I'd always been a rogue, thief, and—"

"Assassin?" asked the young, handsome druid, speaking for the first time. He turned his head and looked directly at Esar-Haden.

"Brother Chulainn," said Brother Daveth.

"No," said Esar-Haden, "he's right. I've taken on such jobs. I'm not proud of it, but I have."

Chulainn once more turned and looked out of the window.

"I decided to add adventurer to my list of exploits." Esar-Haden laughed in an attempt to break the tense mood that now gripped the room. "If only I had known just how blinding the sun is, I would have stayed below. It's taken me years to get used to it."

"Tell them why you were in the dungeon," said Sir Gilroy. He tore free a chunk of bread, sopped up a bit of gravy from his plate, and took a healthy bite.

"As you may know," said Esar-Haden, "the King has kept his kingdom in war for almost the whole of his reign." There was grumbling from both knights and druids upon hearing this remark.

"As you may also know he's spent an egregious amount on his palace. I've never personally seen it but I hear it's the definition of opulence. Such things aren't had for free.

"If you recall," continued Esar-Haden, "when the King's father died unexpectedly there was a power struggle. The Queen-Mother was accused of betraying military secrets to the enemy. She was kept under lock and key for some months. All the while our young King was denied her love, counsel, and protection. The matter was cleared up but it made an impression on the King. He remained suspicious of the nobles and leery of the power they held.

"When you add these ingredients together what you get is a need to acquire gold and a desire to take it from the nobility. By this you strengthen the throne and weaken those striving to take it." Esar-Haden smiled.

"This has never been done. Yet the King wished it. He set about looking for tax men with stiff enough spines to carry out the job. He found few applicants. After all, the nobility would not give up their gold willingly. It was the source of their power. Many feared that death would be the result of knocking upon those doors—rightfully so.

"I saw an opportunity. The reputation of my race precedes me. I have avoided many a scuffle on account of my dark skin, white hair, and my race's bloodthirsty reputation, nary having to unsheathe my daggers at all. I wasn't afraid of country squires. They were afraid of me. What better man to collect taxes?

"The King agreed, or at least those he'd tasked with the hire. So off I went to grab bags of gold. If a few coins happen to tumble out and land in my pocket, well, what's the problem with that? After all, it's theft all around, isn't it? Theft by the crown, theft by me. Anyone who steals for a living knows that those who help him steal are going to steal from him in the process—it's expected."

"Except the King didn't think so," said Sir Gilroy. "He loosed the Sheriff on you."

Esar-Haden titled his head. "He's new to knavery." This brought laughs from the knights. "He'll get the hang of it, in time."

"*You* were expected to hang?" asked Sir Jory.

Esar-Haden nodded, smiled, and reached out to pat Sir Gilroy on the shoulder. "Saved at the last minute by a knight in shining armor."

Sir Gilroy *humphed* at that distinction.

"By the authority of the Order of—" Esar-Haden paused, for Chulainn had risen and turned to face the room. "The Silver Hand," finished Esar-Haden, releasing Sir Gilroy's shoulder.

Chulainn stepped to the right and just behind Brother Daveth, who looked up. Their gazes met. Chulainn nodded. Both men looked at Esar-Haden.

"Do you know why you're here?" asked Chulainn.

"My savior remained tight-lipped on that account," said Esar-Haden.

"I shall be concise, as time is of the essence," began Chulainn. "Ever since I was a boy I have suffered a premonition of my own death."

Esar-Haden glanced at the faces of those seated around the table. It was apparent that they all knew this about Chulainn. Brothers Lewis and Darren frowned, for it pained them to think of what must come. The knights were resolved. Brother Daveth was the only one not looking at Chulainn. His eyes studied Esar-Haden.

"I performed a divination in which I begged Morrigan to show me my future. I now know the place and cause of my death. You, Esar-Haden, kill me." Chulainn fell silent. The druids and knights turned to look at Esar-Haden, as if expecting him to mount a defense at such a horrible accusation.

"Why would I do that?"

"I cannot say why. I only know that you're there, with us, when we confront a wizard by the name of Artain Geddes."

Esar-Haden couldn't help but chuckle. "Why would I do that?"

Chulainn glanced at Sir Gilroy then returned his gaze to Esar-Haden. "I understand that you're motivated by the same sins that motivate the people you've abandoned: greed, lust, and gluttony. We can offer you nothing as far as the later two are concerned, but we can appease your greed. You join us because we pay you."

"Except I kill you?"

"Brother Chulainn," said Sir Reginald. "It is not well that you speak to him of these things. You have told him that he turns his blades on you. He may never have thought of doing so if you'd remained—"

"You doubt Morrigan?" asked Chulainn.

Sir Reginald jerked as if struck. "I would never doubt —"

"Then what will come will come, Sir Reginald," said Chulainn. "Esar-Haden, the druids of the sacred grove and the Order of the Silver Hand offer you a job. We need a sell-sword. We are going to locate and attack the wizard Artain Geddes. We need your blades. Name your price."

Sir Gilroy looked at Esar-Haden. "What say you?"

"May I ask a few questions?"

Chulainn nodded.

Esar-Haden sat back. "You knew this, that I kill you. I don't know that myself, but if you say Morrigan showed it to you I'll believe it. You sent your knights out to find me and bring me back. You say that together we confront this wizard, what's his, oh, yes, Artain Geddes. I've never heard of him but—" He shrugged his shoulders.

"I was set to be hanged. Sir Gilroy absconded with me, earning my eternal gratitude. I'm a dark elf. I come from a people that do not have a word for that emotion in their language. If it was a dark elf that performed the divination you had, and if the results were the same, I would be dead. Sir Gilroy, his dark elf equivalent that is, would have killed me while I was chained to the dungeon wall.

"So, you can imagine that this is all a bit much for me to believe." He held up his hands. "Not that I'm doubting your sincerity, but I have to ask—why not just kill me? It's what I would do."

"Because," said Chulainn, "one's fate cannot be denied."

"My people don't have a word for love, either. But, when I was in Pwyll, I was in love with a woman named Soléne. She was a wizard. She tried to teach me magic. I struggled to focus. If you could see her you'd know why. However, I was interested in the school of divination. It seemed a useful school for one in my line of work. Think of how nice it would be to know if my mark had locked and barred the door, or had a hound trained and ready, or a trap set with a poisoned dart. I was motivated to learn these spells. Sadly, she told me that the school of divination was not so clear. It was like looking through a fog, at times. The more distant or vague the thing you sought the denser the fog.

"I don't know if I'm describing it right but the point is such magic requires interpretation. What if you misinterpreted Morrigan's message?"

"What your lover said is true," said Chulainn. "But there was no mistaking the visions the goddess sent."

Esar-Haden frowned. "What can you tell me about Artain Geddes?"

"He's powerful," said Chulainn.

"How many knights and druids are we taking along?" asked Esar-Haden.

"We've forty knights," said Sir Reginald. "Half of us shall go. The other half shall remain here, to protect the druids and the sacred grove, as we've sworn to do."

"No druids shall accompany you," said Brother Darren. "Our place is within the sacred grove."

"This Artain Geddes," began Esar-Haden. "Does he have a fortress, a tower, a standing army, a bunch of magical beasts ready to devour us?"

Esar-Haden saw that the knights all share a look of concern.

"That has yet to be determined," said Chulainn. "Once you accept the job I shall perform another divination. Then we shall know what dangers we face."

"Look," said Esar-Haden. "I'm not going to attempt to argue you out of believing a goddess. I'm not *that* persuasive. But I've battled powerful wizards before. I'm lucky to be alive. If you give a wizard a chance to prepare, if you let him stack his scrolls and polish the gems on his enchanted rings, you have no chance.

"Twenty knights charging across the field of battle makes quite a commotion. I'm not so sure that's the best way to approach this. You called me an assassin. It's true. It's also true you want to hire me. Why don't you hire me to be an assassin. Tell me where this guy Artain is, let me scout the place out, get to know him and his routine. Let me find a weakness—there's always a weakness. Then I'll turn my blades on him."

"No," said Chulainn.

"No?" asked Esar-Haden. He glanced at Sir Gilroy then back at Chulainn. "I mean—"

"You join the knights and myself," said Chulainn. "We attack Artain Geddes. That's the job. Name your price."

"What if *I* say no?"

"You don't," said Chulainn, "you say yes."

Esar-Haden looked at Sir Gilroy. "By the authority of the Order of the Silver Hand, am I right?" Sir Gilroy did not smile. Esar-Haden looked at Chulainn. "As far as my price, I don't know. I've never quoted a price to my victims."

Chulainn walked the length of the table and stood to the side of Esar-Haden, looking down. "Think about it. I perform my divination when the moon reaches its zenith." With this said he left the room.

. . .

Keir awoke with a start. The damp, cold cloth which had been on his brow fell into his lap when he sat up. He knew at once he was in his room at the *Elephant's Tusks Inn*.

The mid-morning sun was shining through the closed curtains, creating wavering bars of gold that fell across the bed in which he lie. He could hear the chatter of the staff preparing the common room below. He could smell the mingled aromas of the coming lunch. He had no idea how he'd gotten here.

"Easy," said Fagan Red-Banner. "You nearly died. That spell—"

"Artain? Where is he?"

Fagan, who was seated next to the bed, bent forward and plucked the damp cloth from the blanket. He dipped it in a bowl on the bedside table and wrung it out.

"Better keep away from him."

"I can't."

"He doesn't seem to enjoy your company."

Keir lay back—sitting up caused excruciating pain in his abdomen—and turned his head to look at the dwarf.

"You brought me here?"

"Aye."

"Why?"

"Safer than the palace. Artain has people there: spies, loyalist, hanger-ons. One of them may try to earn his gratitude by finishing what that spell started."

Keir looked up at the ceiling. "He needs me alive."

Fagan sat back. "So that's why the potions?"

Keir looked at him. "Just after he hit you with black magic, he gave you some white—healing, that is. I thought he was trying to avoid murdering someone on the palace grounds. The King wouldn't take too kindly to that. Then I found—" He pointed to the stoppered vial with its iridescent red liquid. He'd set it on the bedside table just incase he needed it. "I almost gave it to you. But you seem to be coming along better than expected."

"I'm far more durable than I appear," said Keir. "I've Artain to thank for that."

"What is it with you two? You're too young to be his son, although I know he enjoys a lady's company. Are you his grandson? If so, why is he trying to kill you, or not kill you? None of it makes sense to the casual observer."

Keir smiled. "No, it wouldn't." He looked at Fagan. "Thank you."

Fagan raised a bushy eyebrow.

"For bringing me here, for nursing me. You put yourself out. You didn't have to do that."

Fagan scratched his chin beneath his beard. "Well, I like you. Even though we haven't talked over much I have a good feel for people. You're different than the usual rabble I deal with." He smiled, as he meant the nobility and the King's courtiers—all scum in his opinion. "When a dwarf makes a friend—" He bent and patted Keir on the knee.

"Fagan?"

"Huh?"

"Where is he?"

"What if he changes his mind? What if he decides he wants to kill you?"

"I'm not that fortunate."

Fagan frowned. "His country estate. You caught him as he was leaving."

"How far?"

Fagan sighed. "I don't think—"

"I need to talk to him."

"You've done that. Look at the results."

"I'm going to try a different approach."

"Which is?"

"Don't know yet."

"Well, you aren't going anywhere in your condition," said Fagan. "If you notice, I've undressed you. I had to, on account of all the blood. Not to be overly familiar with another man, but if you lift the blanket you'll see that between your knees and your belly button you're in sorry shape."

"I can feel it."

"If you think you're getting in the saddle, or riding in a carriage, or even walking—" Fagan shook his head. He reached for the potion.

"No," said Keir. "Not yet."

Fagan raised an eyebrow.

"I have a feeling I'm going to need it later."

"When you *talk* to him again?"

"Something like that," said Keir. "Now, my friend, if you don't mind, and as the pain is agonizing, I'm going to take a little nap."

Fagan laughed. "That's the first sensible thing you've said."

Preparation

"Fagan?" asked Keir, waking.

"Damn," mumbled Fagan. "Dwarves can't be quiet, no matter how hard we try."

Keir lifted his head from the pillow. Fagan was at the door, his hand on the pull. He turned and looked at Keir. Burnished bronze rays came through the window, lending the dwarf's red beard a healthy sheen. "It's about time you went back to work," said Keir, "instead of sitting here watching me sleep."

Fagan smiled. "Eh, I was sleeping myself. The wine here isn't what I'm used to but it got the job done." He walked to Keir's bedside. "I'm going to fetch Ryel and bring him here. I should have taken you to him but I was thinking only of getting you to safety."

"Don't waste his time."

"Come now," said Fagan. "I thought you were more resilient—"

"I need to borrow three silver."

"What for?"

"The stable boy."

"Been contemplating your debts, have you?" asked Fagan. "Strange thing to do in your condition."

"I'm going to Artain."

"If you get in the saddle," growled Fagan, "the only destination you'll reach is the *Otherworld*. Arawn will find you face down in the dirt."

"I can make it," said Keir, sitting up. He winced.

"Artain called you a fool. He's right."

Keir looked at Fagan. "He would know. Still, I must go to him."

"You've gotten worse. You're bleeding internally. Even I've figured that out. You need Ryel. You need to stay in bed. What you *don't* need is the saddle or another blast of black magic. Drink that potion and go back to sleep."

Keir returned his head to the pillow. "No time."

"Drink that potion. I'll fetch Ryel. All you've got is time."

Keir turned to Fagan. "I wish that were true. Now that they've found the dark elf, matters will progress quickly." He looked up at the ceiling, really looking with his mind's eye at Chulainn. "They're already on the move."

. . .

Twenty knights of the Order of the Silver Hand, Chulainn, and Esar-Haden arrived at a dense forest grove a few miles from Artain's country estate.

"Where's he going?" asked Esar-Haden as he dismounted. Sir Gilroy, who was also dismounting, glanced at Chulainn.

"Talk to the fey."

"He should take some men with him."

Sir Gilroy looked at Esar-Haden. "He's a druid. He's safer in there than out here with us."

"Artain could have magical beasts in there. We're probably on his land."

"What's with you and magical beasts?" asked Sir Gilroy.

Esar-Haden's eyes followed Chulainn as he disappeared into the shadowed wood. "Fought too many of 'em."

"Oh? We've time. Tell me."

Esar-Haden turned to Sir Gilroy. "I'm not one to brag." Gilroy burst out in laughter. Several of his fellow knights looked at him. He covered his mouth.

The squires—each knight had at least one—began to set up camp, gather firewood, and prepare dinner. Gilroy and the other knights went over their armor and weapons, making all the necessary preparations.

"Talk to him," said Esar-Haden to Sir Gilroy, who took a seat on a fallen log and looked up at the dark elf. "You can convince him."

"Of what?"

"To let me do what he hired me to do, to kill Artain."

"Patience, dark elf. That's why we're here."

Esar-Haden shook his head. "Yes, but we're doing it the most dangerous way possible. You've got the perfect tool. Send me—alone. Talk to him."

Sir Gilroy glanced to the wood, then looked up at Esar-Haden. "It's fate."

"It's fate that I kill him?"

Sir Gilroy nodded.

"I'm *not* going to kill him."

"Don't you believe the gods? They control men's destinies, even yours."

"My people worship demons. Even the few of my race that worship the evil gods don't believe they control their destinies. They just want a reward for servitude—and few prohibitions to obey."

Sir Gilroy set his sword across his lap, pulled his water skin over, and dribbled some water onto the blade. He dug his whetstone from his pack and began to sharpen his sword. The sound of the dull scrape irritated Esar-Haden, but not more than Gilroy's attitude.

"Men," said Gilroy, not looking up. "Think they plot the courses of their own lives. Maybe this is true at times or when small matters are concerned. But the gods are wiser than us, they see the grand design, and they direct us as need be." He looked up at Esar-Haden. "Most men are ignorant of this. We've wise druids among us so we know more about the minds of the gods than most."

"The gods sure have done a shit job in my case."

Sir Gilroy managed to keep his laughter subdued. He looked at his sword then set it aside and placed his hands on his knees. "We're going into glorious battle, dark elf. We've got a worthy foe. What more could you ask of the gods?"

Esar-Haden looked at Gilroy, unsure if he was being serious or not. It appeared that he was. "I don't know, wine, women, song, a good night's sleep in a soft bed. A pile of gold to spend when you wake."

Sir Gilroy stood and placed a hand on Esar-Haden's shoulder. "I'd rather serve the gods. They'll be pleasure enough in Annwn. Arawn is a great hunter. There's no greater cause for celebration than a successful hunt."

"Hunting wizards is dangerous."

"Come now, all of life is a danger," said Sir Gilroy, throwing his arm over Esar-Haden's shoulders. "We eat soon, not too much, mind you, or you'll be sluggish tomorrow."

"Yeah, I got a lot of killing to do, don't I?"

. . .

I hated being home, although I use the term home in the loosest sense. I relished every opportunity to leave on errands. I would find my way to the west side of Pwyll, to a part of town called the "Ghetto of White Skin."

This moniker came from the foreigners and surface dwellers with their light skin, so unlike the ebony skin of dark elves. This was the only part of Pwyll allowed to surface dwellers. It was also the only part of town lit enough for them to see. It was there that I found friendship and camaraderie. It was there that I could laugh and find some small bit of happiness.

The older boys tucked away in those filthy alleys were quick with tall-tales about their exploits. A few had run away from home and lived on the streets, begging and thieving. They risked it all.

If they got caught and returned to their mothers, they were in for a beating that would take them to the edge of death. If their mothers were tired of their shit the boys might be sent to Maljamir, never to be seen or heard from again.

I saw these boys as real men. I put them on a pedestal because of their courage. I wanted to emulate them. I wanted to be free, living by my wits, risking it all for adventure. I couldn't see their fear. I didn't know a damn bit better than to worship these sorry whelps.

I picked up all sorts of "bad habits" from these boys. Worst of all I picked up the desire to be free, to have adventure, to run wild and do whatever I wanted. Just like the sorry boys I worshipped, I wanted to escape my miserable fate. I didn't know it was possible to jump one fate simply to end up with a worse one.

. . .

"You and your spell book," said Sir Gilroy, arriving to stand over Esar-Haden, two plates full of food held in his hands. He extended one to Esar-Haden, who set aside his journal.

"I really do know a few spells," said Esar-Haden.

"The jailer didn't seem to think so," said Gilroy, sitting.

"I didn't want to scare the poor guy."

Sir Gilroy was about to speak when he heard a noise and turned. Chulainn was emerging from the grove.

"Good to see you made it back out," said Esar-Haden to Chulainn, who accepted a plate from a squire and sat by the fire that Esar-Haden, Sir Gilroy, and several other knights shared.

The rest of the knights sat around two other fires, little talk between them, for their thoughts were on the morrow. The squires moved about in a bustle, serving the knights and feeding the horses. Chulainn did not look up or respond. "I'd hate to lose my kill," added Esar-Haden. This brought an annoyed glance from Chulainn, nothing more.

"Now's your chance, Chulainn," said Esar-Haden. "Make the right choice. Send me in there. I'll get our man —lay his severed head right here." Esar-Haden patted the ground.

"No," said Chulainn.

Esar-Haden glanced at Sir Gilroy, who held his gaze a moment before looking at his plate of food. Esar-Haden turned back to Chulainn. "At least let me scout. We need to know what we're walking into."

Chulainn did not look up as he spoke. "The fey have told me everything we need to know." He looked at Sir Gilroy. "The plan holds." Sir Gilroy nodded in response.

Esar-Haden shut his lips tight for fear of saying something he'd regret. After a moment he spoke. "I didn't hear of any plan." Chulainn glanced at him, met his eyes, then looked down but did not speak. Esar-Haden continued. "No soldiers? No constructs, a golem perchance? No demonic hounds to nip at our ankles?"

"He makes no use of such things," said Sir Gilroy.

Esar-Haden looked at Gilroy. "That's a bit strange, isn't it? He's so powerful and rich, is he? And yet he's got what, a maid and a butler on the payroll? Is that all?"

"He has no need of more," said Chulainn.

"How can you be so certain?" asked Esar-Haden.

"The fey," said Chulainn. "They have ways of knowing and can be trusted."

"I thought they played tricks on people."

"They do," said Chulainn, setting his plate aside. "One has to know their ways—I do."

"Lucky for us, huh?"

"Esar," said Sir Gilroy. "Enough."

Esar-Haden turned to Sir Gilroy. "So what's the plan then, eh?"

"We get up before the sun," answered Sir Gilroy, a note of martial pride in his voice. "We go to the manor house, kick in the door, drag Artain out of bed and slay him."

"You know what I like about that plan?" asked Esar-Haden, turning from Gilroy to Chulainn. "Nothing."

Chulainn looked up, met Esar-Haden's gaze, then looked back down.

. . .

Keir was riding as hard as he could. He was guiding his horse by moonlight, trusting Fagan's directions. He had to stop. Tears filled his eyes, blinding him. The muscles of his abdomen cramped. He reached into his pocket, yanking free the iridescent red potion that Artain had given him. It sparkled in the moonlight. He paused, fighting the urge to drink it.

"I'm a cracked vessel," he said, wiping the tears from his eyes with the back of his fist, the potion clutched within. "If he has to choose, and he will, he'll take Chulainn."

The horse took one step forward, causing Keir to shift in the saddle. The movement brought so much pain he almost fainted. Only by sheer power of will did he fight off the encroaching darkness. He bent and dry heaved, his throat constricting. He spit out the bit of bile that had come up.

He was worried. He knew he could push himself hard, that his body was capable of much, but he had gone too far. For the first time in his life he feared not erasure, but death.

"Almost," he growled. "It's almost over. I just have to hold out a little longer."

He stood in the stirrups, stuffed the potion into his pocket, and snapped the reins against the horse's neck.

. . .

I was growing increasingly rebellious. My mother and eldest sister, Loci, were distracted. An important noble house had sucked them up and set them to some task that took all of their attention.

My middle sister, Hydeia, was struggling with her studies and spent every waking hour receiving some sort of tutelage. That left Yolandi and the various house servants—what a motley bunch they were—to keep an eye on me.

Yolandi was immature and flighty. I had grown bigger and stronger. I was becoming more of a challenge to control. Without her elders to turn to she had little recourse when I defied her. It was so embarrassing, I think, for her to be defied by me, that she decided to pretend that I didn't exist.

I was spending more and more time in the alleys of the "White Skin." Foreigners, surface dwellers, merchants, and travelers, all took up quarters in the Ghetto of White Skin. They brought with them their cultures and their vices.

There were burlesque shows in tawdry, cramped theaters. There were ribald comedians who mocked the culture of the dark elves. If a priestess ever heard the jokes and insults, she would have had the speakers executed. I loved their foolish daring.

I took my first drink of alcohol in the White Skin. I got into my first fight. I kissed my first girl. Oh, the girls, let me tell you.

The daughters of the most important and aloof noble houses used to slum it in the Skin. Their presence made it dangerous for the rest of us. If anything happened to them we would all be in for it, rounded up and executed. The entire Skin would have been destroyed.

Despite the constant danger associated with these beauties, we back alley boys were intoxicated by them. We let them win at dice, we stole for them, tried to impress them with our daring, risked it all for them, we felt like we had royalty in our midst and it did a real job on our heads.

It was at this time that I fell in with a gang of boys like me, the useless males from low houses. I was one of the youngest. We were "led" by an older boy named Kalam. He was a real slick character. He was attending the military academy but he snuck out to drink, gamble, steal, and socialize with us. Having ended up in academy myself, I cannot fathom how he managed to get away from that place so often and so easily.

These were good days and I remember them fondly. Since you know that fate has no kindness for me you can guess what these good days led to. The fun and games, the coin, booze, and women, they would all be washed out by pain, misery and suffering. Every good thing comes to an end and it may be a long stretch of bad before you see some good again.

. . .

Esar-Haden looked up from his journal. He listened. Most of the knights and squires were asleep. He could hear their rhythmic breathing. Even Chulainn was curled up under a blanket. The bright orange of the flames had dwindled down to a deep red glow. A quintet of squires kept guard, but their attention was directed outward, away from the camp.

He set aside his journal and rose to his feet. Some night-loving animal made a noise and the squires turned in unison. Esar-Haden slipped away, holding his daggers still so they wouldn't knock against his thighs.

He started toward the grove but paused. He knew there were fey within. He worried they might alert Chulainn that he was passing through their realm. He changed direction and skirted the edge of the wood, careful to avoid fallen branches and hidden stones. He heard movement and paused, listening. His hands slid to the handles of his daggers.

"Dark elf?"

Esar-Haden crouched and searched the wood, then the tall grass to his left. He knew the voice, but he was surprised to hear it. Also, his keen ears had picked up the note of pain within. He saw Chulainn.

"Don't try to stop me," he said. "You know—" The figure stepped closer. It wasn't Chulainn. He wasn't wearing a light blue robe, but a set of well-tailored but worn clothes, the dark sheen of fresh blood, which had soaked through, reflected the moon's light. His skin was pale almost to translucence, his cheeks were sallow, and his eyes bloodshot.

"You're not Chulainn," said Esar-Haden. "But you look—"

"My name is Keir. You're the dark elf from Morrigan's prophecy." He motioned. "Now you're going to assault Artain's estate—you and the knights."

"No, I'm going in alone. Wait, how do you—"

Keir started to speak but collapsed instead. Esar-Haden rushed to him. "You've lost a lot of blood." He started to scoop up Keir, desiring to return him to camp where, he hoped, he could he helped.

"You can't go alone," said Keir, grabbing Esar-Haden's arm. "You won't survive."

"You don't know—"

"I know how this will play out. There's only one way to stop Artain."

"I've got to get you to camp."

"No," said Keir. "You've got to assault the manor house. You must confront Artain." Keir saw the doubt in Esar-Haden's eyes. "I've thought it all—" He coughed up blood. He didn't bother to wipe it from his lips but continued. "I know exactly what he'll do."

"Artain?"

"Listen and do exactly as I tell you. You must not fail."

. . .

Sir Gilroy got up to pee. He stopped by Esar-Haden's bedroll and looked down. He was pleased to see that the dark elf was asleep. Esar-Haden opened one eye and winked. He closed his eye, once more appearing lost to sleep. Sir Gilroy shook his head and walked to the edge of camp.

Struggle

A savage kick burst the door from its hinges, throwing it back into the shadowed interior of the front hall. The knights of the Order of the Silver Hand rushed into Artain's country estate, having already trampled his front garden to mud. Chulainn and Esar-Haden were dismounting as the last man disappeared within.

Esar-Haden could see them through the windows: knocking over furniture, crashing into artwork, spilling vases which shattered with loud cracks. This vision of mayhem was accompanied by grunts and barked commands.

He went to the door just in time to see a maid come running into the room. She saw the knights, screamed, and fainted. A knight caught her and laid her aside. This done, he ran up the grand staircase.

Esar-Haden and Chulainn followed. The staff and residents of the house—Artain was entertaining guests, who now regretted accepting his invitation—were awake and crying out in confusion and fear. A few guards—roused to action by the screams—made an attempt to oppose the knights but were knocked on their heads and tossed into corners.

By the time Esar-Haden and Chulainn mounted the stairs and arrived before the master suite, there was no battle to be had.

"Is he—" asked Chulainn, squeezing his way into the large and lavishly appointed master bedroom.

Sir Gilroy elbowed his way through the knights, arriving before Chulainn. "Empty." He motioned. "Bed's empty."

"He's fled," said Chulainn.

Sir Gilroy nodded. "Search the house!" he commanded, moved Chulainn aside, and led the men from the room. Esar-Haden didn't follow—he listened.

"Chulainn," said Esar-Haden. "Hear that?"

Chulainn paused and listened but his hearing wasn't as keen as the dark elf's. All he could hear were the knights on the stairs. He looked at Esar-Haden and shook his head.

"Casting," said Esar-Haden as he went to an open window. "There!" He pointed.

Artain was on the back lawn. He had discarded his nightgown and stood naked and shivering in the pre-dawn cold. His limbs were spindly, his flesh pale, and he was hunched over with age and infirmity. His thin, white hair blew in the breeze. A trail of footprints in the dew led from the house to where he now stood.

Despite the pathetic figure he made, his voice resounded with power and authority. He moved his hands in an intricate pattern. He turned toward the manor house and looked up. His eyes were rolled back, showing only the whites.

"No!" cried Chulainn.

Esar-Haden grabbed his arm. "What spell?"

Chulainn glanced at Esar-Haden, his eyes wide.

"Damn it," growled Esar-Haden. He leaned out of the window, aimed his hand crossbow, and pulled the trigger. A poison-tipped dart flew across the intervening space but fell short of Artain. Esar-Haden came back into the room. Artain completed his spell. As he did so his voice rose loud enough to rattle the windows.

Esar-Haden and Chulainn watched as Artain fell to his knees, clutching his abdomen. Several knights burst out of the back door and started across the lawn. They skidded to a halt as Artain fell and began to writhe in agony. His screams were horrifying, for the tenor of them was inhuman.

"What in the Nine Hells is he doing?" asked Esar-Haden.

"I don't know!" cried Chulainn.

Artain's body swelled with unnatural lumps, as if he were being filled with tumors. Esar-Haden heard bones breaking, muscles tearing. The sight of Artain's contortions was ghastly.

Artain's legs began to take on the length and thickness of tree trunks. His arms and torso were quick to follow. He swelled to the size of a giant. As his arms and legs grew they cut furrows in the damp earth. The lumps, which were knotted muscles, not tumors, smoothed out.

Artain quadrupled in size. His head swelled too, losing the angularity of age, becoming big and misshapen, like the head of a hill giant. He stood, flexed his massive arms, and laughed. Just like his words had, the booming laugh shook the windows.

"Damn it, Chulainn!" growled Esar-Haden. "That's why he doesn't need an army!" Esar-Haden turned and rushed out of room, bound down the stairs, and ran outside. Chulainn followed. The rest of the knights emerged from the house and formed a loose semi-circle before Artain.

The knights were stunned but rallied and charged forward. Artain bent and swept out an arm but the knights weren't close enough. His fist tore the earth, throwing huge clods high into the air.

Artain laughed and stood his full height. He lifted one massive foot and tried to stomp on a knight, who dodged at the last second. When Artain slammed his foot down the ground shook.

Esar-Haden ran close and fired his hand crossbow, having reloaded it on the stairs. He doubted the poison would do anything to Artain now that he was so huge. The dosage was meant for a normal-sized man, not a giant. Still, he had to try. The dart struck Artain's thigh, but there was no response. Esar-Haden doubted Artain had even felt it. He hooked his crossbow on his belt and drew his daggers. As soon as he had them in hand he realized how useless they would be. At most he could administer pinpricks. He had an idea.

"Tendons! Cut his tendons!" Esar-Haden wove his way through the knights, who themselves were surrounding Artain. They struggled to get close enough to strike, fearing the stomps of his feet or the pounding of his fists.

Esar-Haden made his way to Sir Gilroy's side. "Cut his tendons!" Sir Gilroy looked at him. A wide sweep of Artain's arms caused the pair to dive apart, both landing on their stomachs. His face was close. He leered, laughed, and stood. His beard was like a cascade of white wool. Each pec muscle was the size and shape of a barrel, each quadricep the thickness of a horse.

Artain grabbed a knight by the head, lifted him from the ground, and squeezed. The audible pop as the knight's head burst was sickening. Blood and gore ran between Artain's fingers. He tossed the corpse behind him. It landed, twitched, and sprout a jet of blood from the headless neck.

Artain tried to speak, to taunt the knights, but his words came out distorted and strange. He tried again but it appeared the power of intelligible speech was lost to him. He growled and began to stomp in a wide circle, trying to crush the knights beneath his feet.

Sir Gilroy stood, grabbed Esar-Haden by the shoulder, and yanked him to his feet. "His tendons!" yelled Gilroy to his fellow knights. "Slash his tendons!"

Upon hearing this Artain balled his right fist and brought it down. Gilroy shoved Esar-Haden to the side, leaping the opposite way. Artain's fist blasted the space between them, leaving a deep depression.

Esar-Haden rolled to his feet, turned and rushed away. He spotted Chulainn and went to him. "He can't cast!" yelled Esar-Haden. He arrived beside Chulainn. "He can't cast. It's our only advantage. What can you do to him?"

"I—"

"Damn it, we can't cut him down! Look at him! But you can hit him with something. Think!"

Chulainn nodded and cycled through the spells he knew. He closed his eyes and began to chant. His voice grew loud. Esar-Haden heard a growl that sounded like a tree being ripped from its roots. It was Artain. He heard Chulainn's words of power and was now stomping toward the pair. The knights were slashing at his legs but Artain ignored them.

"Damn it," said Esar-Haden. He looked at Chulainn then at the charging giant. "Come on, come on!" He looked back and forth. Artain lifted his arm over his head, his fist like a boulder launched from a catapult, racing toward them with menacing speed. He changed his mind and opened his hand. He didn't want to smash Chulainn, but to grab him. He brought his hand down in a wide sweep.

Esar-Haden shoved hard against Chulainn, who fell flat on his back a few feet away. When he struck the ground the air left his lungs. The spell was lost. Esar-Haden tried to leap over Artain's enormous hand—it was all he could do—but the palm struck him and he went flying.

Esar-Haden was awoken by pain. He knew at once that several ribs were broken. He couldn't move his left arm, he couldn't even feel it. He felt a sharp pain his right knee and ankle. He tried to sit up but his vision dimmed and he fell back.

He regained consciousness again to a strange taste on his tongue. His entire body tingled. He felt as if he were floating. He opened his eyes and saw Keir kneeling over him, holding an empty vial in his hand. The sounds of battle came to him. He sat up.

Most of the knights were dead or dying. Only a handful remained. They rallied around Sir Gilroy and charged Artain, who himself was wounded.

His legs were coated in blood. His lower thighs and calves were crisscrossed by deep cuts. In several places his shin bones could be seen through open wounds. His arms, too, from the elbow down were slick with blood. With every beat of his enormous heart spurts of blood shot from a dozen deep wounds.

Esar-Haden started to rise. Keir's hand on his chest stopped him.

"You know what you must do."

Esar-Haden looked at Keir. If anything, he looked worse than he had the previous night. His skin was translucent, his cheeks were hollow, his eyes were red with blood. His lips were ashen. The effects of long suffering were etched into his features.

"You're dying," said Esar-Haden. He looked down at his own body. He realized he could feel his left arm again. His ribs no longer hurt. "You healed me?"

Keir attempted a smile. "Artain healed you." He held out the empty vial.

"Where's yours?" asked Esar-Haden.

"I only had one."

"You healed *me*? But you're—"

"Dying? Maybe, maybe not." Keir glanced at Artain and the knights. He pointed. Esar-Haden looked. Chulainn was kneeling next to a fallen knight, pressing his hands against the knight's chest, trying to stop the man's lifeblood from pouring out. "Artain won't attack him. He can't. But Chulainn won't cast. He's too concerned with the knights." Keir looked at Esar-Haden. "He's distracted. He's weak. He can't see what must be done."

Esar-Haden looked at Artain, then Chulainn, then back to Keir. He heard a scream and turned. A knight staggered to the side, fell, and remained motionless. Again Esar-Haden tried to rise. Again Keir restrained him.

"He's hurt—Artain," said Keir. "The knights have cut him deep, but that's not it. He could survive even those wounds. It was the spell. He shouldn't have used such a powerful spell. It's too much for his old body. He won't survive it."

"Isn't that what you want?" asked Esar-Haden.

Keir looked at him. "Once he defeats the knights he'll abandon his body. He won't choose me. Look at me. I've played a dangerous game. I may still lose, even though—" He glanced at Artain. "No, he'll choose Chulainn." Keir looked at his twin. "That's the only time he'll be vulnerable." He turned back to Esar-Haden. "He'll have to fight Chulainn for it, evict him from his own brain. He'll win that contest, of that I'm certain. But as they struggle both will be weak and distracted. That's when you strike. That's—"

"What if he's stronger than you think? He could—"

"Impossible," said Keir. "Chulainn can only oppose him, not defeat him." Another scream. Another knight's death. "Be ready. You must not strike too soon or too late."

"I told you. I'm not killing Chulainn!"

"I'm not asking you to!" screamed Keir. "I'm asking you to kill Artain!"

Another scream, this one different. Both Keir and Esar-Haden looked. The knights were down, even Sir Gilroy. Several writhed in agony. Most were still. The iron odor of blood saturated the air. The scream had come from Chulainn. Artain's giant form fell to one knee. His eyes rolled back and he fell flat on his face, crushing several knights beneath him. Keir toppled when the ground shook. He fell next to Esar-Haden, looking up at the sky through half-open, bloodshot eyes.

"Please." His voice was a whisper. "I beg you."

Esar-Haden got his feet under him and rose, crouching next to Keir. He felt for his daggers but they weren't in their sheaths. He looked and saw one lying several feet away.

Chulainn walked on his knees, his hands gripping the sides of his head, his eyes shut tight. He was screaming, what were meant to be words emerged as sounds of agony. He tried to stand and run but only staggered and fell once more to his knees.

"Get out of my head!" he screamed.

Esar-Haden scooped up his dagger as he ran. He watched Chulainn, searching for any sign that he'd fought off Artain. There was none—only the signs of struggle.

Esar-Haden arrived at Chulainn and grabbed his shoulder. "Fight! Damn you! Fight him!"

"No!" screamed Chulainn, pounding his fists against his temples. "Get out! Get out!"

"Chulainn, listen to me!" screamed Esar-Haden. "You have to fight! You have to—"

Chulainn screamed then fell silent. His arms fell to his sides. He was still on his knees. He began to sway back and forth.

Esar-Haden glanced at Keir. He was lying on his back, motionless. He looked down at Chulainn and raised his dagger.

"Esar! No!" cried Sir Gilroy. He rolled onto his side and propped himself up on one elbow. His hair was caked with blood. Blood was splattered across his face. He reached out with his other hand toward Esar-Haden.

Esar-Haden looked into Chulainn's face. A hardness overcame his features. A foreign light crept into his eyes. Esar hesitated, thought of Keir's words, then plunged his dagger into Chulainn's chest—burying the blade in his heart.

Chulainn's eyes opened wide. He tried to scream but blood poured out of his mouth instead of sound. Esar-Haden yanked free his dagger, dropped it, and grabbed Chulainn's shoulders. He eased him onto his back. Chulainn's lifeless eyes stared up at him.

Esar-Haden heard sobbing. He ran to Sir Gilroy, knelt, and began to assess his wounds.

"How could you?" asked Gilroy, his voice wet with tears. "He was—"

"It wasn't Chulainn," said Esar-Haden. "It was Artain."

"You bastard! I should have left you to hang!"

"Listen to me, damn it! It was Artain. Chulainn was already gone."

"You killed him in cold blood. He was defenseless." Sir Gilroy reached out and grabbed Esar-Haden's arm, squeezing with all his remaining strength. "You coward!"

"Stop fighting," said Esar-Haden. "I have to roll you over. I have to bandage—"

"Let me die!" cried Gilroy. "Kill me! Finish your foul work, dark elf!"

"Stop it," said Esar-Haden. "I didn't kill Chulainn! He was already dead!"

"I saw you! I saw you do it! Just like Morrigan said." Sir Gilroy beat his fist against his chest. "Why did we listen to him? We should have—" He did not finish but gave himself over to sobbing.

"I need to—" Esar-Haden struggled to turn Sir Gilroy onto his back. "You're bleeding."

"Leave me to die!"

"I'm not letting you throw your life away!"

"I failed him," said Gilroy, sobbing. "My oath! My duty! I was going to stop you."

"*We* failed him," said Esar-Haden. "We all did. But we stopped Artain. We'll have to live with—"

"I don't want to live!" cried Sir Gilroy. "Kill me, assassin, I beg you!"

"I'm not killing you. I'm saving you."

Sir Gilroy tried to fight off Esar-Haden's aid but he couldn't, he was too hurt and exhausted. He closed his eyes and allowed himself to be saved, although he couldn't stop crying.

Once Esar-Haden had bandaged Sir Gilroy's wounds, using scraps of torn tabards, he stood and went to Keir. He knelt next to him. "It's over. He's dead. Artain, he's—" He looked into Keir's face. He didn't continue, as the light in Keir's eyes was gone.

. . .

Esar-Haden helped Sir Gilroy to his horse, the larger man's arm over his shoulders, the knight limping alongside the smaller elf, holding his busted ribs with his other arm.

"Why didn't you let me die, damn you?"

Esar-Haden looked at Sir Gilroy. "My life was meant to be a throw away. The only male born to a low house. My fate was to serve the matron mothers and die when they were done with me." He looked over his shoulder, thinking of Chulainn and Keir, although he couldn't see them. He looked back at Gilroy. "It was the same with them. They knew it, just like I did. I didn't accept it. They didn't either. They fought like hell. We all did. You didn't fail them, Gilroy. You fought valiantly. That's all any of us can do."

Appendix One: The Religion of the Celts

For this story I borrowed from the mythos of the Celtic people. What are the core beliefs of the religion of the Celts? Who are their gods?

The Celts practiced both polytheism and animism. They had numerous gods and goddesses, many associated with the natural world and natural phenomena. The Celts believed that the natural world was alive with spirits. Many of these spirits have made their way into the fantasy genre and are familiar to us, even if we aren't certain of their origins.

The Celts believed in what they called the *Otherworld*. This was a realm of magic, parallel to their own, in which the gods, spirits, and dead resided. It was not considered a paradise or a place of punishment, but a world of magic—both helpful and harmful. The *Otherworld* could be reached via portals in caves, rivers, hilltops, and other natural features.

The Celts were attuned to the cycles of the natural world. These played a role in their mythology. Themes of birth, death, rebirth, and the cycles of the seasons were important. Indeed, their mythology featured a plethora of sacred symbols related to nature and the seasons: animals of many types, trees—especially the oak, yew, and ash (all representative of the world tree that connected natural and supernatural realms)—and celestial bodies, all of which held great importance.

The following is a short list of prominent gods and goddesses:

Dagda, known as the "Good God," and the "Dozen King," was a father-figure deity embodying abundance, fertility, and wisdom. He could split himself into a dozen separate embodiments. He wielded an enchanted club that could kill or revive with a single hit, and owned a cauldron of plenty. He is considered the leader of the Celtic pantheon.

Morrigan, a goddess embodying war, fate, and sovereignty. She often appeared as a crow. She could influence the outcomes of battles and was associated with prophecy and shapeshifting.

Brigid, a goddess of poetry, healing, and smith-crafts. She represented inspiration, hearth, and home.

Lugh was a skilled warrior and craftsman. He was known as the "Long-Arm," for his expertise with a spear. He embodied kingship, skill, and light.

Rhiannon was a goddess who embodied sovereignty and was associated with the *Otherworld*. She is also associated with endurance, mystery, and horses, including magical steeds.

Arawn was the ruler of Annwn, the *Otherworld*. He is a god of death and the hunt. He is fair and noble.

Cerridwen was a goddess. She embodied transformation, wisdom, and inspiration. She possesses an enchanted cauldron that she uses for divination.

Cernunnos, often called the "Horned God," was associated with nature, fertility, and animals.

Epona was a goddess and protector of horses, travelers, and the fertile, whether man or beast.

The spiritual lives of the Celts were led by the druids. They conducted religious rituals, which included sacrifices and festivals like *Samhain* (marking the end of the harvest and the thinning of the veil to the *Otherworld*) or *Beltane* (celebrating fertility and renewal). They interpreted omens and signs in order to discover the will of the gods.

The druids were also the keepers of knowledge, both sacred and mundane. This included the oral traditions, myths, laws, history, and genealogies of the Celtic peoples.

Due to their learning, the druids were respected for their wisdom. They often acted as judges, advisers, and mediators.

Druids were associated with the natural world, especially forest groves, rivers, lakes, and other natural environments.

H. Rad Bethlen has been compared to Isak Dinesen (*Seven Gothic Tales*) and Fritz Leiber (*Swords and Deviltry*). He is known for his work in the fantasy and horror genres as well as his non-fiction. He has been published in Europe and America.

Enjoy the story?

If you liked what you read, please take a moment to **leave a review on Amazon**! Your feedback helps other readers find this story. It only takes a minute but it makes a huge difference. The Amazon algorithm requires 30-50 reviews before it will pick this book up and promote it to like-minded readers. Your review is instrumental in helping that happen!

www.ingramcontent.com/pod-product-compliance
Lightning Source LLC
LaVergne TN
LVHW011047110826
845149LV00015B/3381

* 9 7 8 1 9 6 5 6 5 0 3 9 4 *